DAVID COULDREY

THE

FALL

OF

CHARLIE

DIXON

Matador
9 Priory Business Park
Kibworth Beauchamp
Leicester LE8 0RX, UK
Tel: (+44) 116 279 2299
Fax: (+44) 116 279 2277
Email: books@troubador.co.uk
Web: www.troubador.co.uk/matador

ISBN 978 1780883 120

British Library Cataloguing in Publication Data.
A catalogue record for this book is available from the British Library.

Typeset by Troubador Publishing Ltd, Leicester, UK

Matador is an imprint of Troubador Publishing Ltd

Printed and bound in the UK by TJ International, Padstow, Cornwall

THE
FALL
OF
CHARLIE
DIXON

PART ONE

PART ONE

CHAPTER ONE

You know how it is at Christmas. The snow glistens, the church bells toll, the presents lie neatly wrapped under the beautifully decorated tree. And everyone's ripping each other's heads off. You know how it is. You forget how much Mum nags, how hard of hearing Great-Auntie Audrey is, how annoying the little brats running around are, how much of an effort it is to peel two hundred Brussels sprouts that no one even likes anyway. And as always, alcohol fuels and soothes these irritations and fuck it, it's Boxing Day tomorrow, just grab another glass and fill her up; brandy, vodka, champagne, gin, beer, wine, whisky, sherry – and a big, wooden spoon to stir them all together.

James and Christine Dixon were celebrating their first Christmas as man and wife having been married in a touching ceremony at Wandsworth Town Hall in the dying summer of 1987. The happy couple were joined by James' recently widowed mother and mother-in-law, his brother and his brother's two seven-year-old children whose mothers were not invited for logistical reasons. By the time lunch was served, there had occurred fourteen minor rows, three major arguments and two adults and one child had been moved to tears by the spectacle. They had consumed six bottles of champagne, six bottles of red wine, four bottles of white, half a bottle of gin, half a bottle of sherry and a bottle of brandy lay in ambush in the butter on the table.

You know how it is at Christmas.

'Church was absolutely *divine* this morning,' asserted James' mother from behind her heaped plate.

'Surely that's the whole point of it,' James sniped, fingering his cutlery. 'I've told you a thousand times, Christine and I are atheists. When are you going to accept that? Can we please just celebrate Christmas civilly?'

'Don't you think that it's a little hypocritical to celebrate the birth of Christ, if you don't believe in him? If you don't believe he was God's son who died to save us, if you don't believe he was born of the Virgin Mary, if...' Mrs Dixon was interrupted by a snort of derision from the direction of her daughter-in-law. 'Have you got something to say, Christine? Something more to poison the mind of my dear, sweet boy against the Lord our God?'

Christine hesitated before answering but, spurred on by alcohol and fired up by the arguments of the morning, she skewered a potato from her plate and waving it around violently, replied, 'James has always shared my views. For us, Christmas is a holiday and not about the birth of some bastard whose mother got knocked up out of wedlock.' Gravity overpowered her frantically gesticulating arms and as the dizzy potato splashed into the gravy, she prayed that the silence she had created would last forever.

It didn't.

'You horrible little cow,' screamed Mrs Dixon.

'How dare you scream at my daughter like that,' screamed Christine's mother.

'Can you please stop fucking screaming,' screamed James' brother.

'Daddy said the F-word, Daddy said the F-Word,' screamed the kids.

'Christ, I hate Christmas,' sighed James.

'You don't even have to mean it. Just one little word, "Sorry". I hate seeing you two fight.' It was the same conversation that James always had whenever Mother and Wife met, even at the touching ceremony at Wandsworth Town Hall. Christine sat on the bed facing away from him, rubbing the bruised knee that had collided with the dining table in the haste of her retreat.

'That's right, take her side as always.'

James carefully approached his wife and tried putting an arm around her shoulder in the kind of half-hearted embrace that has already acknowledged its impending rebuttal. Finding his arm simply shrugged off, he gambled and decided to sweep her hair aside and kiss her where neck and shoulder-blade meet. This was a fairly large step too far.

She swung round and violently pushed him away before tripping herself and following his falling body to the carpet. Here they remained for no more than an instant, interlocked in a position so obviously conducive to sex that, in that moment, the rules of engagement changed and they began furiously tearing at clothes, spitting, hissing, cursing and both oblivious to the scene downstairs of their family looking up at a trembling ceiling before hastily deciding to clear the table.

Flustered and looking dishevelled, James entered the room where his family were waiting. The two kids were not there but James' mother, his widowed mother-in-law and his brother all looked up at his triumphant and delighted face.

'It's a boy! Perfectly healthy! Ten fingers, ten toes! You can see him in a minute!'

Congratulations echoed from all around and all embraced the joy of new life. For new life, even new life conceived in fury, is umbilically linked to joy. It is the respite from the travails of old life and yet old life does not maintain its love of new life. It embraces it, protects it and then over-protects it. Old life shields new life, keeps it prisoner in the long established ideals of old life and then recoils from new life when it tries to escape. The two become so embittered and alienated that neither can truly recognise the other. They cannot work together but they must. And then the bitter irony: new life becomes old life and the cycle is repeated.

New life is swiftly and unceremoniously scrubbed clean and placed in a transparent box. It is ogled at:

'He has some of his grandfather in him,' sobs Christine's mother.

'He looks so much like James as well,' breathes James' mother, embracing Christine's mother and slyly using her sleeve as a handkerchief. James, who privately thinks that his new son looks most like his exhausted wife, quickly double checks that he isn't the father of triplets or of some by-product of his wife's cravings for micro-chips during her pregnancy. Beauty, it seems, truly is in the eye of the beholder. 'And this is me, this is an extension of me, this is mine,' thinks James.

James sat on Christine's bed, tenderly stroking her sweaty brow as she smiled back at him and thumbed his cheek. They looked up as James' mother shuffled across the room towards them.

'Have you had any more thoughts on names?'

'Well, we were decided on Jenny if it had been a girl, but we were unsure for a boy. We liked Bobby but he just doesn't look like a Bobby to me. He looks more like a…'

'Charlie,' murmured Christine, 'he looks like a Charlie.'

'He does look like a Charlie,' agreed James.

'Well, Charles seems like a lovely name,' chirped James' mother.

James wandered over to his son, cradled him in his arms and brought him over to his mother. The proud parents admired their son. A tiny face with wisps of brown hair crowning it looked back at them with a bizarre expression of apathetic curiosity.

'Welcome to the world, Charlie.'

CHAPTER TWO

Charlie had surprised his parents on the morning of that second Sunday of September in 1988. He had expressed his eager intentions to enter this world five days early just as James' mother, who had been staying to 'lend a hand', was about to leave for church. It has since been uttered, in conspiratorial whispers, that it was in fact the presence of James' mother that had induced the early labour. The birth was protracted and complicated; as if Charlie had had second thoughts about this world before deciding to finally accept its calling. He caused poor Christine fourteen hours of great distress although, being Christine, she didn't mind at all.

The new family stayed in Wandsworth and it remained just the three of them. James and Christine repeatedly tried for another child, but it simply wasn't to be. James continued his tiresome work as a city banker at the same firm where his father had been a senior partner. Unsurprisingly, he had risen steadily through the ranks since joining fresh out of university. James hated his job. He was good at it and it afforded him a comfortable lifestyle but it was certainly not the path he had dreamed of in his youth. He had wanted to study philosophy at university but was financially persuaded by his parents that a business and economics degree would be much more useful.

When James met Christine, she had just written an article for a left-wing magazine, viciously attacking the ethical practices of James' firm and finding herself the subject of a law suit. They met in the canteen on the first day of the trial and bonded instantly over their mutual contempt for the firm where James worked and James fell in love with this gracefully ageing hippy who had never and would never surrender like he did. By the time Christine and the magazine were acquitted, they were officially an item, much to the displeasure of James' colleagues and his mother. Christine left the magazine shortly after to become a freelance reviewer, which proved useful after Charlie arrived as she worked from home and she could be with her boy.

Time passed quickly. Toddlerhood flashed by. Charlie had his first haircut, his first Christmas (at which he was one of the few not to cry) and took his first shaky steps. Charlie found his feet quickly, though speech came slower. It was not until eighteen months had passed that he managed his first word, pointing at himself and saying, 'Chilli'. Close enough.

He had the child's trait; the innocence that breeds fearlessness and, as with most children, he adapted quickly and boldly to the new tasks assigned to him: spending the day at nursery away from his mother, using the toilet, learning the alphabet. Modest accomplishments, comfortably achieved. He had also, thus far, resisted his paternal grandmother's lure of religion. She even employed the old tactic of indulgences. Sweets, toys and even once, when Charlie was just four, a crisp five pound note. On his own, he walked down to the local shop and ingenuously tried, though ultimately unsuccessfully, to give the shopkeeper the money as he had seen his father do. Despite all his grandmother's efforts, the only part of the religion he embraced were the stories of Noah's Ark and Jonah and the Whale. He liked animals.

Things continued in the same manner for a number of years, with Charlie's development resembling the majority of boys of that age. James and Christine couldn't believe how fast time was passing and soon Charlie was approaching eleven years of age and his first term of secondary school.

Charlie settled quickly. The first week of school was enjoyable, he was one more step up the ladder and there were a whole host of new faces. Charlie was sure he would make some great friends and whatever worries James and Christine might have held for their son in another new environment were quickly allayed. The wonder in which he held his new environment easily overpowered whatever trepidation he felt. Coming back from his first day of school he casually let them know that he had invited his entire class to what had been planned as a low-key birthday party on Wandsworth Common that coming Saturday. To James and Christine's initial amusement, the guest-list swelled as the week drew on and they were soon given an estimate of twenty kids to cater for.

In fact it was nearer to forty all told. James hastily drove to the nearest supermarket for more supplies while Christine had them all sit down in a big circle and tried, with the help of James' mother and four of the children's parents, to distribute what party food they had prepared.

Kids are mischievous and Charlie dutifully recognised the opportunity that the absence of his father had created. It didn't take much to light the fuse and sure enough, after Charlie and a few accomplices had shaken the bottles of the fizzy drinks and innocently asked the adults for their help in opening them, chaos ensued.

Party food was flying around to the sound of high-pitched laughter, screams and shouts. A piece of chocolate cake splattered against Christine's cheek while a jammy dodger flew past the ear of Charlie's grandmother. Charlie himself sported a variety of facial stains and a huge grin as he hurled a fistful of jelly into the fray. James saw the chaos from afar and sprinted across the common, forgetting the fresh ammunition he carried in his hands. He arrived at the skirmish and was immediately besieged by a gang of eight of Charlie's friends who won from him the fresh supplies and went about ripping open the contents and joyously showering the group with crisps and dips and other tasty morsels.

James recovered himself and noticing his mother looking tired and pale, yelled for silence and order. A hitherto unknown authority in his voice saw him obeyed and there was silence as a yoghurt pot, thrown by a late reactor, sailed through the air and exploded across the chest of his cashmere jumper. James' mother could be seen shaking her head and muttering to herself, 'the youth of today'.

Order was partially restored and the mess was vaguely cleaned up and James set about organising a game of football, twenty a side. As happens with children's football, the kids – all forty of them – relentlessly chased after the ball. Several giant collisions later and the tears started to flow. James halted the game in expectation of the arrival of the kids' parents. The adults tried as best they could to fix up their charges but as the parents arrived to pick up their dirty, bruised and smiling children, James and Christine bashfully made embarrassed apologies, that were received with a range of good humour, incredulity and outrage.

'So, Charlie,' Christine said to her son as they walked homewards with father and grandmother in tow, 'I hope you enjoyed yourself?'

'It was the best, Mum, thanks,' Charlie replied enthusiastically.

'I think next time, we might try and prepare ourselves a little better, I'm not sure how pleased some of the parents were with the afternoon's events,' declared Christine.

'You just wait for my 18th, Mum,' joked Charlie.

'Oh Jesus,' sighed Christine.

'I heard that,' said James' mother half-heartedly.

CHAPTER THREE

With the rapidly approaching sunset of the millennium, Charlie was brought into direct contact with the cold spectre of death for the first time. Less than a month after his eleventh birthday party, James and Christine sat him down and bluntly pierced his conception of mortality.

'Your grandmother, my mother, is dying,' said James. 'She has cancer and they believe she has only a few months left.'

Charlie was gobsmacked. He thought he should probably cry but his eyes remained as stubbornly dry as the back of his throat had become. The words came out thickly and slowly.

'Is there anything they can do?'

James and Christine silently shook their heads before Christine, with a huge effort that she drew from her love, stroked her husband's hand and said tenderly, 'But we can try and ease her suffering.' She glanced at James, 'We have invited her to stay here until…until the end.'

Charlie didn't get it. He thought:

'I don't get it. Does she hurt? Is she in pain? Is she upset? Can I notice the landmarks of her passage? What should I do? "Ease her suffering"? How? She's dying. Comfort her? She thinks she's going to heaven. Do I? Dunno. Should I adopt her beliefs to see how she feels? They wouldn't be genuine. Should I tell her that she's lived a wonderful life? But what's she done? Well, she brought your father into being. But what's he done? Well, he brought you into being. But what am I going to do? It all seems a bit pointless.'

Charlie is a part of generation 'Why?' He needs to know the logical reason for everything, but not everything has a logical reason. So does that make it worthless? Even I'm doing it now. I don't get it.

Charlie asks his parents, 'What's the point of it all?'

They are in the hospital waiting-room as Charlie's grandmother goes through another check-up, from another doctor hoping for another deadline. James answers his son first, 'Some people, like your grandmother, turn to religion. Others simply say, "I am here, so why should I not be?" There are many reasons,' but James doesn't believe this and his voice trails off.

'What's your reason?' Charlie presses.

'For a long time I didn't have one and for a long time I let life pass me by feeling nothing more than a vague contempt for its futility. But then I met your mother,' he turns to smile at Christine and his voice trails off again. He turns his smile upon Charlie, 'And then, just over eleven years ago in this very building my second reason arrived.'

'Yeah, I get it. Me. Thanks, Dad,' Charlie hurriedly acknowledges. 'So that's enough? Isn't there more?'

Christine smiles at her boy, 'There's as much as you dare to dream for, Charlie. As long as you don't let life break your dreams.' Her voice is steady and certain and hopeful.

'And how do I do that?'

Christine continues to smile. 'That's the real question,' she replies as a door swings open before Charlie's grandmother.

As a seaman might comment on a coming storm, she

states calmly, 'It'll come around soon enough. Probably by the New Year.'

It would be close.

Charlie spent a lot of time with his grandmother in those short months that held the longest of nights. He had learnt much about her that he had never known and had never suspected. Throughout his life, Charlie's grandmother had been for him a periphery figure that flitted in and out of his life at short, regular intervals – birthdays, Christmas and occasional weekends. She had been a figure with whom, understandably, it was not easy for him to relate. She was exactly seventy years his senior – a throwback to a time which simply didn't relate to Charlie's lack of experience of the world.

Charlie's grandmother was born in 1918 and grew up with the fledgling radical ideas of a country freshly brutalised by war and a flu epidemic. She suffered a child's hungry belly in the depression of the thirties and tried to ensure her future security by marrying an almost aristocratic banker on the outbreak of another war. When he returned in 1945, they spawned two baby-boomers who grew up with the fledgling radical ideas of a country freshly brutalised by war and a morality epidemic. She worried with the world as two irresponsible nations led the earth to the brink of destruction and back again just in time. She watched on the television as man walked on the moon. She remembered where she was when, like dominoes, bright lights were felled by evil men. She watched her sons grow outraged at the world they had been born into. She watched their generation cry out against war and hate and injustice and her generation. She watched as her elder son left university unfulfilled and grudgingly followed his father in to the bank. She grieved when, in 1984, her husband died. She told Charlie how she had never recovered from losing him, how he was her love and her life.

Charlie learnt of these things and marvelled incredulously at how such souls had borne all this and wondered if his fledgling soul could stand even a fraction of it. This is the unbreakable human spirit, he thought. She did capitulate to some extent but Charlie sympathised. She had seen injustice and war and poverty and depression and death and she was tired. And so she began to live through religion – zealously.

The curtains were drawn, but the last light of the afternoon still penetrated the beige drapes and cast shadows indiscriminately around the room. One fell over the face of the frail woman in the bed and hid the fatigue that consumed her greying eyes. Her daughter-in-law had brushed her hair but it was thin and brittle and unresponsive to being fashioned. An odour hung around the musty room and its helpless occupant; the unmistakable stench that so ingloriously accompanies the end. The room was quite bare, just a few faded photos in old frames resting inconsequentially on an antiquated dressing-table with a chair that faced away from it and towards the heavily blanketed bed. A lamp shared the small bedside table with a battered old radio and of course there was the old woman, the greying eyes focussing towards the door as her ears strained to confirm what sounded like footsteps coming up the stairs.

There was a knock.

'Come in.' The voice was frighteningly weak and pitiful and yet betrayed the yearning for a little more company, a

16

little more time. It's a rare person who doesn't, when confronted with death not life, desire the prolongation of the end. Why not? It's natural. It's survivalism.

Charlie poked his head round the door, his hair was wet from the rainy walk back from school and he wore his school uniform scruffily, his shirt not tucked in, his tie at half-mast.

'Hey, Gran,' he said. He had replaced the 'Grandmother' on which she had previously insisted as he had come to know her better. He pulled out the chair from the dressing-table and sat down, leaning over to kiss her on the forehead. 'How are you feeling? Anything good on the radio today?'

His grandmother smiled at him. 'I feel the same as yesterday,' she whispered, 'and the radio was much the same as well. Tell me about your day at school.'

'It was pretty good actually. I came top in a test we had and the first edition of the newspaper is nearly ready, we just need a couple more articles. I was thinking of doing one on your life if you didn't mind.'

'My life?'

'Yeah, everything you've told me over the last few weeks has been absolutely fascinating. What a life you lived.'

'I'm still living it, Charlie,' she gently reminded him. She had in turn replaced 'Charles' as she had got to know him better.

'I'm so sorry, Gran, I didn't mean it like that… I just…'

Her eyes almost twinkled. 'It's okay, dear; most fully grown adults put their foot in it much more frequently and cause greater hurt. My life hasn't been fascinating, Charlie, neither has the time in which I have lived. Harrowing maybe, but then again, that does so often create a morbid fascination I suppose. It's hard for you to understand.' Again she smiled gently but even this was a great effort.

Charlie knew she was right. He didn't get it, how could he? They belonged to two different worlds, two different centuries, nearly two different millennia. The divide was colossal and yet here he sat, just inches from the wrinkled, shapeless face that was a part of who he was, albeit an uncertain part.

Charlie hesitated and then resolved to say what he meant to say. And then he didn't. And then he plucked up the courage and before he had a chance to lose it again he asked her, 'Do you think you'll go to heaven?'

His grandmother was not taken aback, she had been waiting for the question and she had her answer prepared.

'It's not for me to decide but do I think there is a heaven? Yes, I do. I look around and amidst the ugliness and the hate that I've seen there is also beauty and love. And then I look upon those that I love and hold dear and recognise the difference they've made to my life. And their reward, I believe, is heaven. I don't think of pearly gates, I think of the house I grew up in, in Kent, and I am surrounded by all those that have gone before me, your grandfather, friends I lost in wars and to disease, they're waiting for me. I have no proof but that is what faith is all about. Do you have any faith, Charlie?'

He faltered, he didn't want to break to her that eleven years of constantly trying to convert him had been a waste of time but he thought she already knew.

'Not really,' he said, 'to be honest, I've been thinking about it in the last few weeks and I simply don't have a clue.'

'That's fine, Charlie, you're young, you'll figure out what works for you.'

'But if each person has something different that works for them, then surely they're all wrong. Or at best, one is right. That's what I don't understand about religion.'

Charlie's grandmother decided to reveal her biggest secret yet. 'To tell you the truth, Charlie, I've been thinking about it a lot over the last few weeks as well and more and more I've realised that it's not the religion I believe in. Each religion is naturally tainted with human error but they carry some good guides to live by, as well as some bad ones. I think all that believe, believe in the same God but the agendas of men have blighted his true prescription. You don't need to follow a doctrine to believe in God. You can even choose to follow what seem to be the sensible guidelines and ignore the rest.

'God without religion?'

'Exactly.'

'I knew the sixties rubbed off on you a bit, Gran!'

Charlie's grandmother faintly smiled but she looked tired and Charlie instructed her to rest for a while. He still didn't get it.

CHAPTER FOUR

Christmas that year was an understandably subdued affair. James' brother and his two children, now both 18 and inseparable, joined James, Christine, Charlie and Charlie's grandmother. Charlie's grandmother managed to get out of bed for the main course of a lunch that she didn't touch until fatigue prompted her withdrawal before dessert. There was little Christmas cheer and not a single argument. It was almost ghostly – a mere shadow of the fiery festivities of former years.

After lunch, the family gathered round the television to watch the same dull rubbish that they show every year. Like the Queen's speech. As the atmosphere became more and more unbearable, James declared that it was time to open presents and went upstairs to see if his mother had the energy to participate.

Charlie and his two cousins brought the presents from beneath the withering tree and up to their Gran's room and arranged some chairs around her bed.

The whole family had had the same conundrum over their Christmas presents. After all, what do you buy for someone who could die that very day? In the end, they gave a joint present of an old record player complete with a stack of classical vinyls. Music soothes all…

In keeping with the glum occasion, the other presents were less lavish than ever, no one felt much like giving or receiving that year except Charlie's grandmother.

With no little effort, the old lady sat up in her bed and asked Charlie to retrieve an envelope from the dressing-table. He found it a lonely item in an otherwise empty drawer and he took it over to his grandmother. The family looked on enquiringly but, pre-empting any questions, Charlie's grandmother withdrew several sheets of paper from the envelope and announced simply, 'This is a copy of my will.'

The family exchanged curious glances as Charlie was given the document and asked to read it aloud.

'"This is the last will and testament of…"'

'Ignore the blurb, Charlie,' instructed his grandmother.

'Okay, Gran, let's see…"To my sons James and Daniel Dixon, I bequeath the proceeds from the sale of my estate in Tunbridge Wells, Kent, to be divided equally between them."' The brothers gave each other an unintelligible nod. '"To my daughter-in-law Christine Dixon, I bequeath all my personal items of jewellery and clothing."' Christine's mouth formed a perfect circle of shock. '"To my grandsons Thomas and Timothy Dixon, I bequeath the sum of £40,000 to be divided equally between them."' The two eighteen-year-olds beheld the other's widened eyes and realised they were millionaires. Charlie had already read the next sentence in his head but read it aloud with the self-consciousness in which he would have read Chaucer.

'"To my grandson Charles Dixon, I bequeath the sum of £100,000 to be used for the sole purpose of paying the tuition fees of Downsouth College, at which he has a place for the school year commencing September 2001. If he chooses not to accept this, he shall receive £20,000 upon attaining the age of eighteen years and the remaining £80,000 shall go to the RSPB."'

Okay then.

Charlie continued with his intonation of uncertainty

as he said, 'Wow thanks, Gran.' His sentiments were echoed by the rest of the family but his grandmother had eyes for him alone.

'Charlie,' she said. He didn't meet her gaze. '*Charlie,*' she repeated more sternly. He looked at those greying eyes and they seemed to wither further under his reluctant stare. 'You have no obligation to accept this proposal. I understand if you want to remain here but I promise you that it will provide a wonderful education and your grandfather, father and uncle would all testify to that.'

Now, it was James and Daniel's turn to look uncertain. Charlie found their expressions and found them wanting. He looked at his grandmother and found her final wish in her eyes. He found himself uncertain, he found no response.

'Think about it,' his grandmother prompted, 'just try and let me know before…'

'I will, Gran,' Charlie said seriously. 'I will.'

But he already knew.

It was New Year's Eve and the old lady hung on. Charlie pretended to have not yet decided and it seemed to him that his apparent indecision had made the old lady worse. She had deteriorated rapidly over those days, and twice a doctor and a priest had been summoned. But she hung on and seemingly waited for Charlie's decision.

If innocence had bred fearlessness then the spectre of death had punctured the breastplate of this fragile armour. Charlie discovered himself to be a coward. He had grown to love his Gran and he didn't have the courage to reject her. His bogus thoughts were interrupted by fireworks from outside. Raucous laughter accompanied his affected pacing of the kitchen. A bottle of champagne on the sideboard knowingly mocked his artificial preoccupations. An unwanted gift. He could relate to that.

He felt so alone and so childish that when Christine silently entered the room and when Charlie looked up to open arms and sympathy, impulse sprung him towards their safety and their comfort and left salty tears and snot on her maternal bosom.

He struggled for breath in each fraction of a second that he wasn't weeping. He wailed inconsolably, 'Why does she have to die, Mum? I love her, it's not fair. Do something, Mum. Please.'

Christine held her son close once more and whispered in his ear, 'I know it's unfair, sweetheart. I know it is darling.'

The dialogue repeated itself several times before Charlie's breathing eased and Christine stepped back, holding him by the shoulders to look at the pain and anguish of her son's face.

'Charlie, what you're feeling is a wonderful thing. I know it doesn't seem like it now, but you're extremely lucky. You'll look back on these months and be so, so thankful for the relationship that you made with her.'

'But it's false, Mum,' he sobbed. 'I don't want to do what she wants me to do. I want to stay here with you and Dad and my friends, I don't want to leave.'

Christine held her son's face and forced his pained eyes to meet her loving ones. 'You are under no obligation, Charlie, she told you that. Simply tell her the truth, that's all we owe to those we love. Nothing more.'

Charlie nodded his head, wiped the tears from his eyes and rubbed his sleeve across his nostrils.

'Shall we go up?' Christine asked tentatively.

'I'll meet you up there in five, Mum, I just need to wash my face first.'

'Okay, darling.'

Charlie reached for the hand towel and it absorbed the fluids of his grief and the softness comforted him. The smell too. He looked in the mirror and tried to penetrate the reflection of his eyes like an apprentice narcissist. They told him nothing of who he was but he continued to search them. They were eyes ragged with grief and completely unconnected to the eleven-year-old face in which they lodged. They were a red and blotchy stain upon his youthful visage. They held the shock of an amateur boxer taking his first hard punch. But he was no warrior and he cowed. He hadn't the arsenal to punch back. At whom?

He replaced the towel upon the rail and carelessly watched it slide off. His fingers dithered upon the lock he slowly pulled back, his other hand a vice upon the door handle. He forced himself through the door and began to walk up the stairs. On the landing he looked longingly back towards the front door of the house but turned left towards his Gran's room.

He didn't bother knocking. Manners are a luxury of time and time there was not. Besides what was he going to intrude on? The old lady lay absolutely still but her pathetic, gasping breaths still dominated the silence. Charlie's father stood at the foot of the bed with Christine's arms draped around him. Compassion emanated from the pair but its direction was unclear.

'Hey, Gran,' he kissed her on the forehead and clasped the hand she tried to hold up for him. 'I've been thinking about what you said,' he hesitated, 'your offer.'

The shapeless face was incapable of creating emotion, but the lower lip somehow fell to reveal bare gums and unshielded saliva. How infantile she looked. Charlie felt old.

'Gran, the thing I've learnt most in the last few weeks is just how much I love you guys. I know that I have to lose you but I don't want to lose Mum and Dad too, I want to stay here. I'm sorry.'

That sad, lower lip drooped further, reservoirs formed at the corner of those eyes, the rasping breathing accelerated, a cough, a convulsion and no one reacted. Feeble but frequent coughs now filled the silence, the hand that gripped Charlie's tightened and pulled the rest of the foetal body round to face him.

'Please.' It was pathetic, born out of a longing to influence a world that no longer belonged to her.

'Please,' she repeated, this time in a voice so frighteningly weak that only Charlie heard her. This was death. This was the end. Charlie continued to hold her hand, stroking his thumb across its unsmooth back, rising over veins, brushing over the wrinkles, and through those hands he felt the end, he became aware that the hand he was holding was not alive but those desperate, pleading eyes still held on and Charlie knew for what they waited.

Anything but this, he thought. What kind of a person denies someone they love their dying wish? Look at her while she waits for your consent; look at the fear in her eyes. Look at her desire for the consolation prize. Look at the lost faith. Look at the squalor of death. Reject it.

'Okay, Gran, I'll go,' he said weakly.

And the words flushed the life out of the old lady, they wrested the glimmer from her eyes and she was still and dead and gone. Charlie returned her hand, glanced at his wide-eyed parents and left the room.

He entered the kitchen and went straight for the champagne bottle. He smashed the neck, raised the jagged edge and cut his lips as the froth coursed through him.

In the hall, his grandfather's grandfather clock struck midnight. It tolled for her and it called her to him while Charlie lay bloody on the floor and a bitter laugh escaped him.

The funeral was the first that Charlie had attended, and it had been planned in great detail by his dearly departed. He helped to carry the coffin into the church and, due to the height discrepancy between him and James with whom he locked arms, he nearly caused it to fall. It was a very heavy, very old coffin and it dug into Charlie's shoulder, leaving a mark. His Gran had curiously chosen it at the time of her husband's death. Maybe there was a discount.

Charlie read a psalm. You know the one. They always roll it out at funerals, 'Though I walk through the valley of the shadow of death', although Charlie didn't get to that bit. He couldn't get the words past the lump of grief and guilt at the back of his throat and James had to finish it for him while Charlie walked past staring eyes, out of the church and into the fresh, Kentish air. He returned to the back of the church after a few minutes and watched the rest of the proceedings from there. The priest said some meaningless words and Charlie scanned the room.

It was a fairly poor attendance, he thought, but then again many of her contemporaries had gone before her. There didn't seem to be many signs of the grief that plagued Charlie across the foreign faces that sat, hands folded in their laps, looking dreamily up at the cleric. He wondered who they all were and what they were doing here.

Charlie finally found amidst the black suits and dresses, a spark of colour. A woman wearing red, near the back of the church, knelt and rocked incessantly. Her face contorted and mascara dripped from her eyes, brushed her cheek and fell to the cold, stone floor of the church.

CHAPTER FIVE

'Charles Dixon?' The man at the front of the class surveyed the room magisterially. He was a well built man in his mid-forties, muscular, with a square jaw and severe eyes that had fleetingly glanced over the owners of those voices who had nervously acknowledged their names. He wore a very well-made dark suit with ostentatious pin-stripes over a light pink shirt with starched collars and what can only be described as the most perfectly triangular knot Charlie had ever seen. His feet were adorned with highly polished black brogues and as he rocked on them laconically while calling out the register, he flashed glimpses of bright red socks.

'Present, but it's Charlie, not Charles, if that's cool.'

'Present but not correct. You will call me either "sir" or Mr Chadwick. What are your tie and your top button doing, Dixon?'

'Some kid yanked on it and I undid my top button to try and undo it but...but I couldn't.' He just remembered in time, 'sir'.

'Come here, Dixon.' Charlie got up and made his way to the front of the class past the apprehensive faces of his classmates. Chadwick began roughly undoing the knotted tie, not paying much regard for the comfort of its captive.

'Where are you from, Dixon?' demanded Chadwick.

'London,' Charlie replied instinctively, as he swayed gracelessly to the whims of his teacher's hands like an unwilling puppet.

'I meant what school did you come from?' said

Chadwick, as he finally managed to release the knot.

'Just my local school in Wandsworth, sir.'

'Then you probably don't know what a "Windsor knot" is, Dixon?'

'No, sir, I don't.'

Chadwick proceeded to tie the elaborate knot that he himself sported. 'Whenever you come to my class, Dixon, you will be wearing a "Windsor knot" and I will not be able to see your top button. Is that understood?' he said as he tightened Charlie's tie to the point of strangulation.

''Sir,' Charlie gasped.

Greatly perturbed, Charlie made to return to his seat but was pulled back by Chadwick who commanded, 'You shall remain at the front for the time being as my scribe. I wish you to write what I dictate on the board.' Turning to the rest of the class, having raced through the register and given Charlie a pen, he said, 'Write down and memorise the following: "This is the first of many things I have learnt at Downsouth College from Mr Chadwick and I will regard it with the utmost importance: Manners Maketh Man."'

New pens scratched on new pads as Charlie wrote on the board. Chadwick surveyed his class contemptuously before turning around to inspect Charlie's copy on the board.

'Are you trying to be funny, Dixon?' he seethed through clenched teeth.

'No, sir, what do you mean?'

'Read what you have written out loud.' Charlie saw it, in bold capitals on the board and his heart sank. One, perhaps two of his classmates let out discreet titters. It read:

MANNERS MASKETH MAN

'Sir, I'm really sorry, I didn't mean to, I wasn't thinking.'

'Detention. Sit down and I warn you that you say another word at your own peril,' hissed Chadwick as his eyes flashed maniacally. As Charlie trudged back to his seat, his mind wandered unhappily to his friends back home, organising their lunchtime plans in overt whispers at the back of the class.

'You have all been fortunate to come to this institution. Some of you,' Chadwick looked at Charlie, 'have been very fortunate indeed. This is a school with a great history and a great tradition. Our list of notable alumni matches that of any school in the country. It was schools like ours that churned out the architects and the guardians of the greatest Empire the world ever knew. We expect greatness from all of our students. As your form teacher for the first year, you directly reflect my performance. *Do not let me down.*'

He looked at a few faces seemingly at random, and once more lingered on Charlie. Charlie tried to return his stare defiantly but it didn't work, he just looked like a scared and lonely boy, who wished more than anything to leave. Chadwick pressed his advantage.

'So…to history. Why do we learn history, Dixon?' he asked.

He had evidently forgotten that he didn't want to hear Charlie's voice but the scared, subservient tone in which he was answered seemed to please him greatly.

'Er, so that we can learn stuff about, um, why or how, er, the world is like it is now?'

'Dixon, you're an absolute genius,' said Chadwick. No voice was ever more tainted with the lowest form of wit.

Chadwick turned to the rest of the class. 'Over the course of this year, we will be learning how Britain came to be Great. We will be learning about Empire and how we, as a nation, brought light to some of the darkest corners of the earth.' Chadwick was relishing his subject and the attention he was being paid and, in no time, he was full swing in to his well rehearsed, jingoistic monologue.

The class remained silent and attentive throughout, but as soon as the bell rang there was a collective din of packing up and moving chairs.

'What the bloody hell do you think you're doing?' roared Chadwick. 'Have you already forgotten the first thing you learnt here today? Do you all want to follow Dixon to detention?' Everyone had stopped like musical statues. 'Go on, get out,' Chadwick hissed.

There was a silent race for the door and Chadwick flashed Charlie a cruel smile as he left. As soon as the class reached the stairs, there was an outbreak of excited talking and someone slapped Charlie on the back sympathetically as they rushed past him, leaving him alone with his thoughts.

The rest of the day wasn't much better. Completely disorientated, Charlie was late to almost every class and with every unsympathetic berating he received, he became more and more daunted by the prospect of the next five years.

And there didn't seem to be any kindred spirits. Most of the boys had been packed away to a boarding school by their parents from an early age. Several boys commented on his inevitably tainted accent and all seemed to have prior friends.

After five demoralising classes, Charlie tried to make

his way to the lunch hall but once more became lost. When he finally arrived, the table at which the new boys sat was full and he made his way over to the only table with empty seats. The occupied ones were holding an eclectic mix of loners, oddballs and late-comers. He would later learn that this was affectionately known as the 'reject table'. Nice.

Head down, he determined to eat the indecipherable shit in front of him in perfect silence. A clatter of chairs and trays made Charlie look up as a slightly older boy noisily sat down next to him. Scraggly brown hair fell freely below his collar and he sported no Windsor knot. He looked at Charlie briefly, who quickly returned his own concentrated stare upon his food.

'New boy, eh? Well, good luck to you, this place is a fucking prison camp. Been back five minutes and that cunt Chadwick has already given me detention.'

Charlie liked him instantly. 'I haven't had the best start to term either. Chadwick gave me detention in the first class and I don't think the other teachers like me much.'

'Ah! You must be the "little shit" he was talking about. My detention was for telling him that whatever you'd said to wind him up, I wholeheartedly agreed with.'

Charlie shrugged shyly and a smile escaped him, 'Thanks, I appreciate the support. I'm Charlie.'

'Well, Charlie, I'm Benny and I've got a bit of advice for you. Don't go winding Chadwick up too much or he'll make your life hell. I've gotta be on my best behaviour for a while now. What'd you do to set him off anyway?'

Charlie explained the whole affair as Benny roared his approval and drew disapproving stares from teachers on distant tables, which he nonchalantly ignored.

'But it was a mistake, I didn't mean to,' explained Charlie.

'Freudian slip more like. I had him for my first ever class too and we had to write down that same bullshit phrase. I much prefer your version.'

'Thanks. So what's the deal here? I feel like I've walked into a completely different planet.'

'My friend, you've just entered a time-machine. In the 400 years or so that this place has been around, it has perpetually struggled to keep pace with the outside world. Chadwick must have told you that it produced "the kind of people that made Britain 'Great'", when the sun never set on the British Empire and the sun never rose for its reluctant subjects. But they swallowed the bullshit then and they're still shovelling it down. The people you see around you are the modern day viceroys, or they think they are. The school just wants to attract the richest clients. It's a business. The way to do that is to top the league tables so it's all about grades. And if they think you're not gonna help that goal they'll tell you where to go.'

At that moment Chadwick walked past their table and gave Charlie a contemptuous snarl. For Benny, however, the look was one of vitriolic hatred and Charlie actually shuddered. Benny smiled pleasantly as Chadwick walked on.

'Wow, he really fucking *hates* you mate,' Charlie told Benny. 'Did you see that look?'

'Yeah, he does. Wanna know why?'

'Go on then.'

'Well…the reason that Chadwick hates me so much is actually because I'm in love with his daughter.'

Charlie nearly exploded. Love? Chadwick's daughter? He looked to Benny for the punch line. Nope, not coming.

His features were serious but they glistened as his mind wandered over the object of his love.

'How on earth did that happen?' Charlie asked as Benny snapped out of his reverie.

'How it normally does, mate. We met and we fell in love. End of. She's everything to me and that's why I plan on sticking around here.'

Charlie was dumbstruck but mostly by that word. Love. What the fuck is that? Benny was enjoying Charlie's awed attention and asked him if he would like to go for a cigarette after lunch.

'Thought you were on your best behaviour?'

'I'm on my best behaviour when it comes to expressing myself in front of teachers. They concede to me my minor victories like smoking myself into an early grave. Although the teachers with slightly too much time on their hands do like Hunting us, it's their modern day badger-baiting. Chadwick's the best Hunter in the school, I'm about the only guy he's never caught.'

'I dunno, I reckon I'm in enough trouble for one day and my folks would flip if I get caught smoking. I'm still only twelve'.

'twelve! I thought you were old for your year. How come you're only twelve?'

'I'm thirteen soon; I'm near the cut-off so I was just bumped up a year a while ago.'

'Don't worry about it, dude, age is just a number. Anyone who can piss off Chadwick like you did is fine by me.'

The rest of lunch was spent with Benny divulging his ultimate tips for survival and Charlie continued to listen intently as they cleared the trays and returned to their table. Shortly, a clattering of chairs preceded a hush, filled by the monotonous voice of the head boy, with a perfect Windsor knot, uttering a soulless grace. The two teachers who flanked him smiled their approval and shook his hand enthusiastically on the completion of his task.

Charlie followed Benny out of the dining-room towards the back of the rabble and jogged after him as he surreptitiously changed direction towards the woods. Checking the coast was clear, they dived into the foliage.

They entered the woods at the top of a steep dirt bank, which Benny charged across at full pace. Charlie tried to follow suit but tripped over a root and caked his uniform with dirt. Benny looked behind him, laughed and carried on running. Charlie followed. After a few minutes they arrived at a barbed wire fence that had been pulled apart enough for Benny and Charlie to pass through. They pushed through a bush and Charlie found himself in a large flat opening with wildly overgrown grass. Under a birch tree there was an old bench and some thirty yards beyond it were an assortment of empty bottles, beer cans and cigarette butts that lay strewn in the undergrowth.

'Looks like they still haven't found this place,' smiled Benny. 'Welcome to the Secret Garden,' he said and sat down on the bench.

'I'm filthy,' Charlie sighed and went about trying to dust off his uniform. 'Where are the others then?'

Three long whistles reached their ears from the direction they had just come from.

'That's them,' smiled Benny. He had taken off his jacket and was now using it as a makeshift cushion on the bench.

'What's the whistling about?' Charlie asked.

'So we know that they're not teachers. You'd be amazed how seriously everyone takes this little game of cat and mouse.'

Three boys entered the opening. One, Charlie was pleased to note, had an equal amount of dirt on his uniform.

'Alright, boys,' Benny welcomed. 'This is Charlie. He's my apprentice!'

Everyone introduced themselves. The kid caked in dirt was another new boy called Tom Leary. The other two, Benny's friends, were Jake Cunningham and Harry Prince. Everyone pulled out a packet of cigarettes except the new boys who had none, but Benny scabbed Charlie and Harry scabbed Tom.

The older boys lit their cigarettes and Benny blew a few smoke rings. Charlie tried to light his but it didn't seem to work. Tom was struggling too.

'You gotta inhale boys,' Benny advised them.

Laughter followed spluttering and when the coughing had died down, Jake spoke.

'Johnny Campbell told me Chadwick gave you detention,' he said to Benny. 'What a cunt.'

'It's this little bastard's fault,' grinned Benny and he proceeded to retell the story of their linked detentions. Jake and Harry cackled throughout while Tom looked on with a hint of jealousy.

'You wanna watch yourself, Charlie,' Harry warned. 'Chadwick's an arsehole and he welcomes any excuse to show his colours.'

'It was a mistake though,' Charlie tried to explain, but Harry had already turned back toward Jake and Benny.

'What a shithole,' he pronounced. 'I can't believe we're back again, man, I already wanna get out.'

'I take it you had a pretty good summer then?' asked Benny.

It sounded pretty good. Harry had been down in

Newquay surfing for the summer and, if he was to be believed, shagging half of Cornwall. Jake had been to Spain with a group of friends, getting pissed every night and having a great time. Benny sounded like he had had the best summer but maybe that was just because he talked the loudest. Charlie decided not to tell them of his summer and they didn't ask. There was nothing to tell anyway. This also seemed to be true of Tom, who Charlie started chatting with.

'So how did they rope you in to coming for a ciggie on your first day?' he asked.

'They said they'd beat me up if I didn't,' Tom replied simply. 'I think they were joking though.'

'Oh.'

'You?'

'Er, much the same.'

'How are you finding it so far?'

'Alright, I suppose, it's just very different to what I'm used to I guess.'

Tom looked relieved. 'Me too, who the fuck are all these pricks saying how their previous school was the best in the country or that 46 members of their family have been through here. Who really gives a shit?'

Charlie laughed and nodded his head appreciatively. 'I know exactly what you mean. As a matter of fact, three of my family have been through here but the two that are left didn't enjoy themselves much, I don't think.'

'So how come you're here then?' Tom asked.

'Well, that's a long story. It was my choice though. Yourself?'

'Scholarship,' Tom grunted, looking embarrassed. 'I just wanted to get away from home to be honest, my parents run a pretty tight ship.'

'From what Benny says, you might have just traded one hard regime for another.'

'Yeah, I'm getting that notion too,' Tom said, coughing a little.

By now, everyone had finished their second cigarette, lit directly from the first, and Benny announced it was time to go. They exited the woods in pairs, and had a small moment of alarm when they saw an adult walking towards them. But it was a gardener and he walked on by.

That Saturday Charlie had his detention. Thankfully, the teacher on duty was not Chadwick but an ancient physics teacher with bad hearing, bad eyesight and absolutely no control. Charlie sat next to Benny at the back of a fairly empty classroom. Evidently, it was not very easy to get detention in the first few days back.

Benny had his laptop out and was playing computer games, with a look of intense concentration that the wizened, old physicist mistook for academic rigour. Charlie periodically watched him play when he got bored of his essay, entitled 'The importance of manners'.

Benny saw him looking at his screen and minimised the game. 'Bored, Charlie?' he whispered. Charlie nodded in acquiescence. 'Check this out.' Benny opened a video file and it took Charlie a minute to realise what he was looking at, in a jumble of orifices and dildos.

'What the fuck are you doing?' he hissed. The teacher at the front looked up briefly and then returned to his marking.

Benny turned up the volume for a fraction of a second and an exaggerated moan of ecstasy filled the room and there was an outburst of laughing.

'What are you all laughing at?' the old man demanded. 'Silence, or I will keep you another hour.'

Charlie and Benny giggled silently.

There were only twenty minutes left and Charlie had to write fast to finish his sycophantic task.

CHAPTER SIX

The Tuesday after Charlie's detention was his thirteenth birthday. It wasn't something he was looking forward to. It would be the first birthday that he hadn't been with his parents and only his second without his grandmother.

His alarm woke him up at seven and he reluctantly got out of bed and went to shower. He got dressed and went over to the dining room for breakfast, where the dinner-lady, a lovely middle-aged woman from Ireland, wished him Happy Birthday. Charlie hadn't a clue how she knew but thanked her and accepted a bowl of oats.

When he returned to his boarding house he found a card waiting for him from his parents and was almost moved to tears as he read it. They hoped he was settling in well and that he was keeping out of trouble. They wished him Happy Birthday and begged him not to live up to the reputation of a terrible teenager. They said that they loved him and were proud of him. They missed him and couldn't wait to see him.

Charlie realised how much he missed and loved them too and paused to look at their photo in his room. He had a lesson with Chadwick directly after chapel and he remembered to tie his Windsor knot for him. He managed to keep his head down for the duration of the class and let the following four classes pass him by passively. When he got to lunch, there was space for him on the table with his year and he duly sat down to join them. Benny, on the reject table, looked disappointed but met Charlie at the scrap bin to wish him Happy Birthday.

'Coming for a smoke after lunch then, birthday boy?'

'Yeah, why not?' Charlie replied.

'You're only three years off the legal age now, boyo,' Benny smiled. 'They grow up so fast,' he crooned and ruffled Charlie's hair.

Charlie pushed him away and politely told him to fuck off.

Jake, Tom and Harry were all there after lunch and they all wished Charlie a happy birthday and each gave him a packet of cigarettes, which Charlie then scabbed back to them. They each smoked three cigarettes consecutively and then exited the woods and went back to their various boarding houses.

When Charlie and Benny entered the common room, it was not to find the whole house noisily watching some Australian soap as usual. The room was full and silent and there were teachers there as well. The brilliant blue sky of a New York fall filled the screen and comprehension dawned on Charlie as he read the text at the bottom of the screen. He looked around the room and saw the shock in everyone's face and as he turned back to look at the screen, the second plane hit.

'Fucking hell.'

'Christ.'

Somebody started crying. It was Jamie Coxon, a fellow new boy who was from New York. 'My Dad,' he stumbled through his sentence, 'he works there. Oh God. Dad, please no.' A teacher swooped on him and led him from the room and away from the television.

Over fifty adolescent boys sat in shock, mesmerised by the horrific images, and anyone who talked, spoke in whispers and only to those directly beside them and Charlie couldn't hear what they were saying. He was thinking of Jamie Coxon and pictured him desperately trying to make contact with his family.

He looked up at the television and saw debris falling from the buildings and then realised that it was not debris but people jumping knowingly to their deaths.

Human empathy does still exist and it poured out of every boy in that room. For some, it was too much and they left. Others, Charlie included, stayed and watched the events unfurl.

Was he watching history or just people dying?

'Charlie, my boy, I've got quite a treat lined up for you.'

Charlie was lost in thought and the deep confusion of incomprehension. He thought of the dead, of the living, of the dead, of the why's, of the dead and of Jamie Coxon and the pain and the dead. He thought of those who jumped. He watched them falling, falling...

'Charlie, wake up, pal. I said I've got a treat for you.' Benny had his hand on his shoulder and peered into Charlie's face as if checking his vital signs.

Charlie emerged from his trance, reached deep for enthusiasm, got half a grip on it and replied, 'I'm all ears, mate, tell me more.'

'Good. How do you fancy a party?'

'A party?'

'A party.'

'A party?' Charlie thought of dancing on graves.

'You know – sex, drugs and rock 'n' roll? A party.'

'Here? Tonight? I don't think it's exactly the right time for a party, Benny. Besides, how the fuck are you gonna pull it off?'

Benny smiled a broad grin and motioned for Charlie to follow him. They arrived at the door to the toilets and

Benny turned to face Charlie triumphantly. He glanced towards the toilet and said, 'My friend, I'm a man with a plan.'

'Well, I'm not consenting', quipped Charlie.

'Very funny, come in.' Benny pushed open the door and began unscrewing the panel beneath the basin. 'What today should have taught you is to live for the moment.' He pulled a bottle of vodka and a bag of weed from the depths of the plumbing. 'You have to seize every opportunity that comes your way,' he said smugly.

Impressed but infuriated by Benny's expression, Charlie said scathingly, 'You mentioned something about sex?'

'And so the lamb becomes the tyger, eh? Well, have a little faith in me. Do you know who I mean by Sally Chadwick?'

'The love of your life?' Charlie mocked.

Benny glared at him. 'The very same,' he said tersely. Charlie made to talk but Benny wasn't finished. 'Her friend Jessie, who I met at the same party, is currently staying with Sally because her parents are out of the country somewhere. And these two lovely girls are meeting us by the athletics track at midnight.'

'Well, fuck me.'

'Here's to hoping,' Benny said as he raised the bottle to his lips and swigged greedily before passing it to Charlie. He drank his first ever vodka and as it burned his throat, he spluttered and saw Benny laughing. With tears streaming down his face, he joined in Benny's savage roar of triumph.

At a quarter to midnight Charlie was standing by his desk fully clothed in his darkened room and waiting for Benny to appear. He was still thinking about the events and the images of the day but he resolved to try and enjoy tonight. He felt fear too and felt guilty for being afraid. He had nothing to be frightened of in comparison to the scores of thousands who felt a purer fear that same day. This was schoolboy stuff, he knew.

Benny didn't bother knocking when he entered and he laughed quietly as Charlie started, looking scared.

'Alright, Chaz, looking forward to our fiesta?' he whispered, shutting the door behind him.

'Yeah, mate,' Charlie replied uncertainly. 'Are we leaving now?'

'In a minute, our dear housemaster's light is still on and I usually like to wait for him to turn it off.'

'I think you might be waiting a while, Jamie Coxon's in there waiting for news.'

'Shit, still no word about his old man?'

Charlie shook his head. 'I don't think so. Obviously they fear the worst.'

'Fuck. Poor kid,' Benny empathised but seemed to put it out of his mind as he shook his head. 'No matter, we'll be alright slipping out the back, just need to brief you quickly. It's your sixteenth birthday.'

'What? It's my thirteenth birthday, Benny.'

'No kid, you're sixteen like me. That's what the girls think,' Benny smiled.

'You're fifteen,' Charlie objected.

'It's just a little white lie, Charlie, *relax*. They're sixteen, or so they told me, and they're not gonna be very interested in a thirteen-year-old are they?'

'Fuck, Benny, I ain't got the experience of a sixteen-year-old, they'll bust me for sure.'

But he had to laugh. Tonight he would be trying to

lose his cherry to a girl he'd never met. Still, it's best to get these things out of the way early. The two youngsters embraced and Benny led the way out of the room and down the back stairs where he pulled off the fire dome over the lock and silently opened the door that swung out into the pitch black of the outside world, the moon hiding helpfully behind a cloud.

Five hundred metres from their boarding house, it was safe to talk and they swigged on the vodka bottle as they made their way across the rugby pitches to the athletics track a further half-kilometre away. Charlie felt braver with every sip and was soon encouraging Benny to light up a spliff.

The athletics track was on a plateau between two slopes and they crossed over it, Charlie crashing noisily into an unseen hurdle en route. The noise of their laughter grew as they finally came to rest, sitting down on the bank of the second slope, completely out of sight from the boarding houses behind them. It was only now that Benny agreed to light a spliff, as its cherry would be blocked by the contours. It was after midnight and the girls hadn't arrived but the boys puffed away merrily and drank heartily their Russian poison. As the spliff burnt down to the roach they lay back on the slope and looked up at the stars that sparsely littered the sky, silently content.

A noise startled them and they crept up the hill to look across the athletics track. They could just about make out two silhouettes, walking towards them, and Benny got out his phone and rang Sally. He heard her phone ring momentarily and hung up immediately, smiling at Charlie in the darkness.

'Here they come, mate. Ready?'

He whistled to the approaching figures and they

accordingly changed their straying path directly towards the waiting males. Charlie felt nervousness and excitement flutter through him, exacerbated by the cannabis and vodka, and before he had fully composed himself, they had arrived. It was nearly half past midnight and the girls most definitely had some catching up to do.

Benny embraced Jessie jovially and kissed Sally tenderly, while Charlie shuffled awkwardly on the slope a foot or two behind him.

'Girls, this is the birthday boy,' he said, indicating Charlie, and both girls swooped upon him and planted kisses on either cheek, wishing him Happy Birthday.

'What took you so long?' Benny asked.

'Dad.' It was Sally who answered. 'He was watching some programme about Kipling on the history channel and we couldn't get away sooner. Clearly you've already started,' she said, surveying the swaying boys who half-fell back in to a sitting position and motioned for the girls to do the same. They handed over the vodka and invited the girls to light up another spliff and soon the party was in full swing.

The girls had brought with them a bottle of Malibu and this was opened and shared and before long both bottles were half empty and a couple of spliffs had been smoked and everyone was well and truly wasted. Charlie was having a wonderful time and he lay now next to Jessie, slurring profusely and asking her about her school. She told him that she had been expelled.

'Why did you get expelled?' Charlie asked.

Jessie giggled. 'You really want to know?'

Charlie rolled over and looked straight into her eyes, 'I really want to know,' he said.

'Well…' she ran her right hand through Charlie's

fringe. 'My friend and I invited some local boys to meet us down by the athletics track to celebrate my sweet sixteenth and we were caught by the deputy headmistress with our knickers down, surrounded by empty bottles and a quarter of an ounce of skunk,' she breathed towards his face, which smelt heavily of booze.

'Oh.'

Jessie giggled once more.

'Really?'

Again she giggled, 'Not really, no. But it's not beyond the realms of possibility, is it?'

And her hand found the back of Charlie's neck and pulled his face towards hers and she parted his lips with her tongue and they kissed. After several minutes and with a slobbering mouth, Charlie extricated himself and looked over towards the entwined shadows of Benny and Sally where audible moans floated towards him.

'Me.' Jessie reminded him and they locked lips once more.

Charlie was nervous. He thought he knew what was coming and was silently praying that he would not disappoint. He had grown hard almost immediately and, like an adult male, started thinking with his dick. It told him to remove Jessie's jumper, which he threw carelessly behind him. He then removed his own hoodie, and felt the cold night air on his bare arms. He kissed Jessie's neck before bringing his head down to where the fleshy, upper parts of her breasts protruded from the strappy top she wore. Presently this was removed and on deciding that she was a little bottom-heavy he thereafter pulled down her jeans, whipped off his shirt and pressed his crotch against hers, pulsating like he'd seen in the movies.

Her hand entered the top of his jeans and found him

ready. Charlie unzipped his trousers and crawled out of them, kissing her all the while. He was getting really nervous now and he fumbled for the clasp of her bra with difficulty before it relinquished, whereupon he pulled it away and her breasts flowed out. He jubilantly started on her nipples while her hand pulled, tugged and stroked his dick as he became more and more excited.

He pulled down his boxers and rolled over, the wet grass indistinguishable from the sweat on his back and Jessie went down on him, slowly at first and then with greater intensity until Charlie became nervous once more that he wouldn't make it to the final hurdle and they rolled once more, Charlie's head ending up between her legs, which he pulled apart before removing her knickers and briefly going down on his first ever fanny.

With his left hand he found the condom in the back pocket of his jeans lying just beside them and he brought it to his mouth which was once more by hers and tore at the wrapper with his teeth, removed the condom and put it on.

Now he was really nervous. He hoped he would find the right hole.

She spread her legs obligingly and thrust her hips skywards and Charlie entered her. For an agonising moment there was no response but as he filled her she moaned and Charlie sensed Benny looking up at him and smiling approvingly. He had no idea what to do, so he just went in and out and out and in and in and out until they rolled over and Jessie sat on him, leaving his preoccupations redundant as she took control. She pivoted and swerved and rocked back and forth and they were together, in unison moaning as silently as possible but with a shortness of breath until Charlie felt the moment that he knew was the end, and she knew it too. And she sat for a minute smiling down at him, kissed him on the lips, playfully nibbled his ear and then stood up.

Having located their strewn garments, Jessie and Charlie rejoined the other two who had already re-robed following their tumble on the hill and were smoking a spliff, Benny holding the last of the vodka and Sally, the Malibu. The bottles were handed over to Jessie and Charlie, the latter also receiving the joint, and they sat down in a square and recommenced shooting the breeze and laughing, until the drink was gone, the joint smoked and they lay down in a line looking up at the stars and chatting shit like veteran stoners.

Eventually, Benny pulled out his phone and seeing that it was past four in the morning, declared that they should go back. They stumbled up the hill and across the track, two-by-two, arms draped around each other for support, whispering meaningless sweet nothings. In the last patch of darkness before the boarding house, Charlie and Benny kissed their girls and watched them walk off into the distance, in the direction of Chadwick's house.

The boys silently re-entered their house, where Benny locked the back door behind them and replaced the fire dome. When they reached the first floor, they embraced, Benny slapped Charlie lightly on the cheek and said, 'See you in the morning, big man,' before continuing up the stairs to his floor.

Charlie entered his room, shaken, dizzy and ecstatic. He regretfully set his alarm for seven-thirty, just three hours hence, quickly stripped again, flopped on to his bed and let sleep engulf him.

Fuck was the first word that sluggishly went through

Charlie's mind. The alarm clock on the desk was ringing and so was his head. Looking at his tormentor, he rolled his eyes and found this painful. He pulled his pillow from beneath him and threw it at the alarm clock, which sent it, still ringing, down the crack at the back of his desk. Mournfully, he rolled out of bed and let himself hit the floor. He crawled under the desk and turned off the clock and brought this and his pillow back to bed with him. He re-set his alarm for fifteen minutes later.

That was fifteen minutes? It felt like two.

Pain engulfed his head and the light of the morning insulted his bleary eyes. His mouth was dry and he chewed his tongue and the sides of his mouth in a futile attempt to bear saliva. His stomach felt delicate and he needed to shit. His mind forced him first to think of Jamie Coxon and of New York and of death and of his grandmother and it was unpleasant and guilty. So this was glory.

He thought momentarily and inconsequentially about how he had sex a few hours earlier. The cold and unforgiving light of day rendered it meaningless. It was. It meant nothing.

He moved his duvet around and his pillows and himself, searching for the comfort that never comes the morning after.

Benny entered, customarily, without knocking. 'Thought you might be struggling, mate,' he grinned, fully dressed, freshly showered, coffees in either hand. This did not help. He leaned on the edge of the desk having given Charlie his coffee.

'How do you feel?'

'Shit.'

'We've got register in twenty minutes, mate. Gulp that down and have a shower. Got some aspirin for you as well,' he said offering it to Charlie with a bottle of water he pulled out of his pocket. Charlie swallowed three pills gratefully.

'Wicked night, mate,' Benny enthused. 'You fucked her, you little stud!'

'Yeah,' Charlie groaned, sipping on his coffee. 'Hope I did it right,' he said massaging his eyebrows.

'Sure you did,' Benny encouraged. 'You need to get yourself ready for register though, otherwise they might suss something. So, I'll see you down there?'

'Sure, mate. Cheers.'

'In a bit.'

'In a bit.'

CHAPTER SEVEN

Tall, dark and handsome, Benny Stone looked like the father he had never met. He had been raised – if you can call it that – by his mother in a luxurious West London apartment. His mother was not yet forty and although life had robbed her of the stunning beauty she had possessed when she had met Benny's father, she was still superficially sexy.

Aged seventeen she had fallen desperately in love with Benny's father, a thirty-something member of the modern gentry. Aged eighteen she married him. Aged nineteen she fell pregnant. And aged twenty she returned home early from a cancelled maternity class to find Benny's father doing some rich whore from behind up against the stove on which she laboured over his meals.

Her heartbreak was instant and instantly induced labour. The guilty lovers became aware of her presence as her waters broke right there in the kitchen and Benny's father, knowing the decent thing to do, put his clothes back on and drove her to the hospital. He even wanted to be present for the birth but she refused and she never saw him again. The birth was tricky and they were forced to operate.

Heartbroken, physically scarred, twenty years old and vocationless, she returned several days later to the luxurious West London apartment that Benny's father, again knowing the decent thing to do, had abandoned. Somehow they both survived. She took solace in the creature that suckled on her breasts. Indeed, Benny fed like this until long after he had learned to walk and talk. As a toddler he would often clamber upon his mother and get his feed as she lay unconscious after a cocktail of painkillers and anti-depressants.

Men came and went. Some never even came – shocked as they were to find beneath silk underwear the damage wreaked by Benny's teeth and the surgeon's knife. Most men faked it but one, when Benny was five, audibly shuddered as he removed her bra and so she started Benny on solid foods and, with all future lovers, refused to let them see her mangled mammaries.

From then on, Benny looked after himself. There was always plenty of money available – his father, knowing the decent thing to do, had provided well for them in the divorce – and Benny took what he needed from his mother's purse while she lay unconscious after a cocktail of painkillers and anti-depressants.

As time passed, Benny's mother – when she was conscious – sadly noted how much Benny was growing to resemble his father. By the time he was twelve, the similarity had grown so strong that she could no longer bear to look at him and she proposed that he go to boarding school the following year. He didn't have to think twice about it before gladly accepting. Even if he had not been in detention most weekends, he would never have gone home to that. It was all so terribly sad.

Despite, or because of, Benny's own traumatic past, he was capable of great compassion. Even, in a way, to Mr Chadwick. Chadwick's recognition of this empathy might well have propelled his intense dislike for his daughter's young love. He knew that Benny knew, you see. How often are we particularly on our guard with the confidants of our own confidants? The unsettling knowledge of the existence of an equal or surpassing intimacy with one who you hold dear. One who knows your joys and tragedies, desires and falls.

And of course Benny knew all about Mr Chadwick because his life was such an integral part of Sally's. They shared not only filial love, but familial misfortune too.

Just a few short years before Benny had come to Downsouth, Richard Chadwick was unrecognisable. He had, it's true, always been a hard man and incredibly driven. He was almost wholly concentrated on his studies and on rugby, but something he had never known crept up on him and he tripped and fell in love.

Stalking the cloisters of a renowned Oxford college and deep in thought on his imperial thesis, he could never have seen the petite brunette with whom he collided and sent sprawling to the stone. Dazed though she was, she was impressed by the solidity of the body into which she had crashed – and the large hand, too, that offered a return to verticality – but it was the glimpse of the tenderly apologetic eyes that stirred her as she got to her feet.

Contrarian justifications for Amritsar fled his mind as he looked down at what appeared to him to be the most beautiful creature he had ever seen. An apology tumbled from his larynx and she reassured him that she was not seriously hurt, although she did feel the need to sit down.

'I know a quaint little tea shop around the corner,' said the big, burly, rugby playing postgraduate, and she smiled, amused, and said that would be lovely thank you very much.

Chadwick went to the loo eight times later that evening for they had drunk six pots of tea together. She had inspired in him a trust that enabled him to tell her things in one afternoon that he had told nobody over the course of a lifetime. And she was fascinated because the human tenderness that remained in his slightly watery eyes did not seem to match the stories he was relating. The truth is that it had only appeared when first her eyes met his and when, many years later, it was extinguished, it left no trace and one would think that it had never been there at all.

Her name was Lucy Black, and she was a remarkable lady. Not in any tangible sense but the change she effected in Richard Chadwick was astonishing. They courted. We don't do that these days. We fuck. But they courted and it was gentle and it was tender. They both had their studies to pursue but every evening they would meet for tea in that quaint little tea shop and on the weekends she would watch him play rugby and they would go punting on the river.

This was the late 1970s but their courtship was largely shaped by Chadwick's whims and was thus very outdated. But although he controlled the mode of their relationship, she soon propelled it to the limits of this fashion. When the rugby season was over and Chadwick had a little more time on his hands, he invited her one weekend to meet his parents.

They loved her. She was dignified but helpful, confident yet respectful, and she uncomplainingly lent her ears to grumpy diatribes against the state of society from Chadwick's father, and the ceaseless worrying of his mother. But they loved her most for loving their son.

They had watched the hard, focussed man grow up and they had feared that no one would be able to penetrate this shell. This was the first girlfriend he had ever had and they were pleased to see the effects; he was softer, gentler, kinder. And it even had an effect on his academic work.

His thesis, when it was finished, had taken a direction that he never envisaged it would. It didn't turn out to be a jingoistic justification for exploitation but a thoughtful, meditative and balanced judgement of British foreign policy in inter-war India.

He didn't attribute this to her and maybe we shouldn't either. Maybe he actually, after thoroughly researching the topic, changed his point of view. Either way, he knew happiness and contentment like he never had before and at the end of the year, when he was her date for the undergraduate ball, they ended up lying on the slanted roof of her college watching the stars and he, with utter certainty, proposed. She, with doubts, accepted.

The wedding was a low-key affair. A few of his Rugby team-mates attended, one of whom was surprised to find himself as best man, and there were a dozen of her friends from school and university. It was a traditional, small, country church wedding and they had a small reception in the village hotel. After, they spent ten days on the Cornish coast for their honeymoon.

With time, she overcame her doubts. The changes in him continued and, in every action, his deep love for her was reflected. And she loved him for being the tender creature he was with her. He became a teacher at a Home Counties grammar school and she became a librarian. It wasn't an exciting life but it was a homely one. The first few years of their marriage were ones of, dare I say it, domestic bliss. In the school holidays, she would take time off work and they would ramble around the British countryside. At first, they explored the Home Counties and then later they went on trips to Yorkshire or Cumbria or the Scottish Highlands.

When Lucy became pregnant with Sally, they thought

their happiness complete. When Sally arrived, a beautiful baby girl, they stayed in the small house they had lived in since he had first taken up his post at the grammar school and their family was complete. They watched little Sally grow up with joy. They dressed her in little flowery numbers and watched her dance around their small garden in the summertime.

Father and daughter were especially close. In truth, he spoilt her but he could not help it for he could not resist her smile and he did everything in his power to keep it as permanently etched on her face as possible. He encouraged and supported her in everything she did and everything she wanted to try.

They watched her become a proficient young tennis player and a popular pupil with staff and students at the primary school. They swelled with pride as members of the community cooed and told them how lucky they were for having such a sweet little girl. She took up musical instruments and helped her mother to bake cakes, a true Little Woman.

But for some reason, life cannot let us be. As with cycles of despair, cycles of happiness break too, and this was a brutal demonstration. Sally was eleven years old and had just started secondary school when she came home one day from school to find her mother complaining of a headache. She instructed her mother to lie down and rest and when Chadwick came home shortly after, he carried her up to bed. The next day, the headache had not passed. They went to the doctor. Within a week, she was dead. Just like that.

Chadwick fell apart. Sally was a brave little girl but she needed to be looked after and Chadwick was in no state to do it. He had extended compassionate leave from his work, while she went back to school a week after Lucy's death. Lacking the support she needed from him at home, she found it in her friends at school. She was utterly devastated but they supported her.

As time passed, Chadwick rebuilt the defences he had erected before he fell for Lucy Black. Slowly but surely, he resurrected a superficial resemblance to his former self. But he was unrecognisable to Sally. Never again would he let someone in as deep as Lucy Black. His heart simply couldn't take it and he backed away from everyone, including his daughter.

He could no longer bear to be in the little house that he had been so happy in and so he applied for new jobs and successfully landed one in the history department of Downsouth College. Sally didn't want to leave the place where her friends were – the friends who had supported her through her grief and who were now, in essence, her family. But she loved her father deeply in a way that he would never again return and she saw that he needed this. So she accepted it with the mature compassion of her mother.

Life at Downsouth was difficult for Sally. She had only her father and he was determinedly disinterested in her. He threw his energies into his teaching and into coaching the school rugby team. She was a day pupil at the girls' school down the road but she wanted to be a boarder. Chadwick refused. He still needed her around even though he refused to engage with her emotionally.

So, once more, Sally took refuge in her other relationships. At St Mary's, she became very close to Jessie and together they went to parties in the houses of posh kids whose parents were away. It was at one of these parties that she met Benny.

CHAPTER EIGHT

When Sally first saw Benny, he was holding forth to three similarly good-looking girls – fake tan, died blonde hair and identical outfits. They were laughing and blushing and batting their eyelids and Benny was visibly pleased with their response.

As she watched him, he swigged from his beer and as he tilted his head back, he saw her looking at him and he froze for a moment, the bottle to his lips, before continuing to entertain the three girls. Sally was talking to Jessie but kept looking over at Benny. He was talking to the girls but kept looking over at her. Whenever their eyes met, one or both of them would quickly look away.

After a while he disentangled himself from the Barbie triplets and walked towards the kitchen. Sally saw him go, made a quick excuse to Jessie and followed him. Benny was alone in the kitchen and didn't hear her come in because he was busy rifling through cupboards.

'Looking for something?' Sally said. Benny spun round with a guilty smile and replied with mock shame.

'I was looking for the parents' liquor.' He grinned. She couldn't help grinning too.

'Did you find any?'

'Not yet, but I remain hopeful.'

Sally opened a door by the fridge that led down to a basement. 'Have you looked down here?' she asked.

Benny shook his head and plunged down into the cellar. Sally followed.

This was what they were looking for. A large cabinet

contained every type of liquor that has ever been invented, or so it seemed to them.

Benny turned, impressed, to Sally. 'Good instincts,' he said.

They began inspecting the bottles, most of which they had never heard of. Those that looked interesting, they opened to smell or have a gulp. Many were disgusting but they had fun trying them out and deceiving each other.

'Try this one, it's delicious!' Sally handed Benny a bottle of green Chartreuse.

'Eurgh! Yuck!' Benny's face contorted as the monks' poison went down.

Eventually they settled on a very expensive and delicious brandy and Benny found a fat Cuban cigar to accompany it. They sat on the stairs of the basement, exchanging the bottle and the cigar between them.

'I don't think you told me your name,' Benny said.

'I'm Sally,' she said.

'Benny,' said Benny. 'Pleasure to meet you,' and he extended his hand for a comically formal handshake.

'Won't your girlfriends be missing you?' Sally asked.

'I dunno what you're talking about,' he smiled. She raised her eyebrows. 'The three Barbie dolls you mean? Just met them tonight. Nope, I don't have a girlfriend me. Single. Definitely single. One hundred percent. You?'

'Same,' she said.

'Interesting,' he said. 'Hmmmmmmmmmm.'

'Hmmmmmmmm,' Sally responded.

He shuffled towards her and she looked away. Hmmmmmmm.

'These guys have got a lot of booze,' Sally ventured.

'Yes they do,' Benny agreed. Hmmmmmmmmmmmm.

'So what school are you at?' Sally asked, dreading the answer.

'Downsouth,' he said. 'Shithole. You?'

'Just down the road,' she replied. 'St Mary's.'

'Hmmmmmmm, so you're very close then.'

'Very. I'm a day girl. I live in Downsouth. My Dad's a teacher there,' she confessed.

'Who is he?'

'Mr Chadwick.'

Benny let out a sound that was half-groan, half-laugh. Sally laughed too. 'I get that a lot,' she said.

'He's a bastard,' said Benny. Sally hit him on the arm.

'Hey, that's my Dad,' she said.

'He's a bastard,' Benny repeated.

'Leave him alone, you don't know what he's been through.'

'Yeah right, I bet he's had a really tough time of it,' Benny proceeded heartlessly.

There was a silence before Sally spoke. 'He was different when my Mum was alive.' She started to cry involuntarily.

'Shit, Sally, I'm sorry. I didn't know.'

'It's not your fault,' she whimpered. 'I just get upset about it sometimes.'

Benny hugged her, 'It's okay,' he said. 'I understand.' And he kind of did. Both he and Sally were emotionally orphaned by parental tragedies and there was something in his voice that convinced her of his empathy.

She dried her eyes. 'Sorry for getting all teary on you,' she said.

'Don't worry about it,' said Benny.

'Thanks,' she said.

She gave him a peck on the cheek and left her face in

front of his. Their eyes stared into each other and there was something there. I can't explain it, I wish I could, but it was something similar to truth. The eyes were drawn closer to each other and then their lips were joined. They pulled apart and smiled tenderly at each other. They kissed again. Again they pulled apart. They kissed again, and the door opened above them. They looked up and Jessie was standing in the doorway.

'*There* you are,' she said to Sally. 'I've been looking everywhere for you.'

So have I, thought Benny.

So Benny and Sally became an item. Because she lived within the confines of Downsouth, they saw plenty of each other – usually in the dead of night when both would sneak out, or on weekends. The relationship developed quickly. It didn't take long for both to realise they were in love and even more surprisingly, they were quick about declaring it too. It wasn't like 'trying to shoot at someone who outdrew you'; they drew at the same time and once they had declared their love, they became ensconced in an impenetrable cocoon.

Nothing could hurt them, for they knew that when the trials of their day were over, they would have each other and perfection was restored. The most beautiful aspect of the relationship was how saving it was. Both of them really, really needed each other.

When Chadwick learned of their relationship, pitifully late, it is fair to say that he was not best pleased. He persecuted Benny with renewed vigour in class and ordered him to stop seeing his daughter. Benny politely declined. Chadwick responded with a string of detentions that only served to keep Benny in school on the weekends, and thus near Sally.

Another of the reasons that Benny was in detention most weekends was that he had struggled to adjust. For so long, he had held the freedom to the city of London and he would run around town on his skateboard like a young urban pirate going wherever the fuck he felt like, but here there were limits. Borders. And Benny didn't react well to this.

His frustration usually found its outlets in petty acts of vandalism and rule-breaking and he was delighted to have Charlie as an accomplice. Albeit, a reluctant one:

'I don't understand why we have to dress the statue of the school's founder in a Ku Klux Klan outfit,' Charlie would groan.

'It reflects the nature of the school,' Benny would counter. 'Besides, it will piss them off shitloads.'

'Do we really need to form the words "Fuck The Headmaster" in the grass with weed killer?'

'You scared, Charlie? It'll be fun, come on.'

'And where are we gonna hide all the hymnbooks once we steal them from the chapel?' he asked.

'We'll dump them in the woods.' Benny said. He always had an answer.

Mostly though, it was just drinking and smoking in the woods. True, they physically escaped the confines of the school from time to time but mostly their escapes took place deep in the woods and their rock hammers and shovels were booze and weed.

Benny was never really a political animal although I concede that there are some who would count anarchy as a political doctrine like those who might count atheism as religious belief. But still, to my mind, Benny was not really political and yet he was instinctively reactionary. And so, in a school that was a hotbed of prejudice and right-wing fervour, he swung left even though he didn't actually know his left from his right.

On Charlie's thirteenth birthday, when New York was attacked, neither he nor Benny had heard of Al Qaeda, Bin Laden or could point to where Afghanistan was on a map. But those things became part of the syllabus for an adolescent of the noughties. It was impossible to grow up in that decade without knowing a little about them. They overshadowed everything.

No one at Downsouth College seemed to have any qualms about going to war in Iraq – it was considered a natural thing to do. But for Benny, prompted by the self-righteous newspaper he subscribed to, it became a cause for his passions. So in February 2003, when all over the world there would be protests against the invasion of Iraq, Benny was desperate to be there. He fancied a nice day out and considered the chances for chaos pretty high.

Needless to say, Charlie wanted to accompany him, and so they got permission to leave school for that weekend in order to exercise their democratic right to peaceful protest. As that week dragged slowly by, they became more and more excited. For the last month they had been in detention every Saturday, which had restricted their freedom somewhat and they were itching to get out of the narrow confines of Downsouth. Finally, it was Friday and tomorrow would be the day of their sally. But today there was one last thing to do.

For all his faults, Benny was a hopeless romantic in his way. Perhaps it was this that appealed to Charlie. Charlie had been enlisted to help Benny in his preparations for Valentine's Day and he could picture in his mind's eye how events were unfurling while he lay awake in bed, excited at tomorrow's trip to London. It was midnight and Benny would now be leading Sally through the woods towards the Secret Garden. He wore black tie and Sally wore a beautiful sapphire dress and in one hand she carried a red rose that Benny had given her when they had met that night.

At the edge of the Secret Garden he would be producing a blindfold and she, with mock nervousness, would let it cover her dancing eyes. He would tell her to stay where she was and rush ahead to light two candles – one that remained on the perfectly laid table and another which he used to see as he quickly pressed play on the CD player and made his way back to Sally as soft music filled the air.

Sally, blindfolded in a sapphire dress beside a bush, would be led towards the table where, as a perfect gentleman, he would help her in to her chair. He would pour her a glass of red wine and remove her blindfold before excusing himself to huddle over a camp stove. She would call him back to give him a kiss.

Not quite a culinary genius, Benny would nevertheless produce a meal of steak and baked beans, followed by pre-bought rich chocolate gateaux. Their conversation is sacred and thus secret but it is enough to say that it jingled with laughter and love.

After they could eat no more, Benny to save on washing up would throw cutlery, crockery and gas stove in to a bush before pouring another glass of wine for Sally over her right shoulder and shrouding her neck in a simple silver chain.

Later, he would offer her his hand and raise her to her feet to dance beneath a starry sky.

CHAPTER NINE

Saturday. They had reached London and were at the protest.

Benny was thoroughly enjoying himself. The volume of noise and people aroused him and he was in great spirits.

'Look at it,' he enthused, 'This is England and people actually give a shit!'

'Do you reckon it'll make a difference though?' asked Charlie.

'Of course it will, mate. You can't ignore this many people and it ain't just London. It's global, bruv.'

'Even I know how cocooned politicians are though, Benny. I bet you they ignore it.'

'Then they're in for revolution,' Benny retorted. 'Look at these people, mate, they are *prime*.'

Charlie grinned at his friend's longing for chaos but shouted loudly above the din of the crowd, 'As if, mate.'

An Asian man in a hoodie with navy trousers and black shoes, who was standing just in front of them, turned round and looked at them curiously.

'What are you looking at?' Benny snarled hostilely, noting the polished shoes.

'Sorry, lads,' the man said, 'I thought you were talking to me. My name's Asif,' he explained.

Benny and Charlie both laughed and the former apologised for his hostility and slickly manoeuvred Asif into the conversation.

'So, you here on your own?' he asked.

'Yeah, I just got off work and thought I'd come down and check it out.'

'What's your work?' asked Charlie.

'I'm a bus driver,' he replied, 'number 238. Worst job in the world; you just drive the same fucking route every single day.'

'I get that bus sometimes,' Charlie said. 'Goes through Wandsworth, doesn't it?'

'That's the one. I park at the big bus shelter in Wandsworth when I finish my shift. I live just round the corner from it actually.'

'Awesome,' Benny interrupted, evidently weary of this Wandsworth bus talk. 'So what do you make of all this then, Asif?' he asked, waving vaguely at the thousands that surrounded them.

'It's an impressive sight,' Asif commented, 'and it's nice to know that people – even young white teenagers like yourselves – actually care what's happening on the other side of the world. Usually young white or black teenagers just get on the bus and call me "paki", he sighed. 'I ain't even Pakistani.'

'Well, you won't get any of that bollocks from us, mate. We should go for a drink when this is over,' smiled Benny.

'It'd be a pleasure.'

The conversation had sagged as Asif and Charlie sat at a table in the corner of the pub. Both were extremely drunk and sat staring contemplatively at the stacked empty pint glasses in front of them, the empty packets of nuts stuffed into the topmost one. Asif's last cigarette was still smoking in the overburdened ashtray and Charlie, whose eyes were stinging from the smoke, fished it out and stubbed it properly. Then he lit a cigarette.

Benny, who had volunteered to go to the bar when the bell for last drinks had sounded, meandered over to the table unsteadily carrying a tray laden with six pints of London Pride.

'They're closing in fifteen minutes, lads, so let's get these down quickly,' he slurred. He was as fucked as the others but Benny had always had this incredible amount of restless energy that Charlie revered and feared. 'Down in one then, lads,' and he drained his first pint. So did Asif while Charlie managed half. And Benny downed his second. His monologue continued. 'I was thinking at the bar – when I wasn't checking out the barmaid that is – that it would be a damn good idea to liberate that Routemaster of yours and drive it back to school.' He seemed pleased with his idea but Charlie wasn't.

'No fucking way,' he managed to object.

But Benny had guessed correctly that Asif's disenchantment with his job and his life combined with the proper measure of alcohol could make him receptive to such an idea. Benny looked at Asif and the devilish sparkle of his eyes persuaded the bus driver. Asif downed his second pint, belched loudly and affirmed his position.

'Fuck,' he belched again, 'yes.'

They both turned to Charlie and again it was Benny's eyes that swayed him – the glint of mischief that had long since conquered Charlie's preoccupations with other misadventures. He downed the other half of his first pint and roughly poured out his second in equal measures for his companions so that they all had something to toast with when he resignedly murmured, 'Fuck it.'

They clunked their glasses, drained the contents and got up to leave the pub. The other two had already reached the door when Charlie swiftly and neatly regurgitated his beer back into his pint glass and hurried after them.

They decided not to take Asif's bus so as not to incriminate him, but Asif showed Benny where the keys to the other buses were kept and Benny broke open the locker and took the first set of keys that impulse guided him to. They located the corresponding bus, an old Routemaster, and as Asif reversed her out Benny and Charlie ran around it like madmen, wildly swigging their bottle of vodka before offering it to Asif who gladly accepted, accidentally beeping the horn as he drunkenly leant over to reach for the bottle.

Asif was very drunk. So was Benny. So was Charlie. And all three of them happily engaged themselves in the pastime of shouting obscenities at the few passing cars. They had just got on the motorway when they heard a siren and their hearts leapt simultaneously until they realised that it sounded for the car behind them that was driving so erratically that the police overlooked the oddity of a London Routemaster leaving the capital at two in the morning. They swerved, bumped and belched their way towards Downsouth College and Benny, feeling sick, decided to retreat to the upper deck and sprawl himself out along the seats at the back. It was the first time that Charlie had ever seen Benny's tireless body overcome.

After less than an hour they had left the motorway and suddenly the school gates loomed toweringly into view. They were locked but Charlie guessed correctly that the back entrance would be open and he directed Asif there. They turned off the lights and crept slowly and stealthily up the hill. When they reached the top, Charlie directed Asif across the first XV rugby pitch and towards the first XI cricket pitch where Asif neatly parked the old bus perfectly over the square in the total darkness that engulfed them. He turned off the engine, pocketed the keys and he and Charlie laughed loudly, slapping hands and congratulating each other on a job well done.

'Go get Benny,' Asif told Charlie. 'We should get out of here quickly.'

Charlie gained the upper deck and drunkenly staggered to the back where Benny lay asleep, snoring softly. He looked so peaceful and innocent asleep. Sleep was the only safe retreat where his demons didn't bother him. But it wasn't for this reason that Charlie didn't rouse him.

However innocent he looked now, it was a facade. Benny had joyously led Charlie into the world of mischief – the world of the noughties – and this was the first time that Charlie had the upper hand in any of their reckless adventures. And now he felt Benny's influence to be a cancer. He wrongly felt that his dissatisfaction with life was in fact Benny's. That the hate and anger belonged to Benny too. But it was his own hate and anger, and his cowardice above all, that caused him to turn his back on Benny, as everyone had turned their back on him, and to softly retreat down the stairs without waking him. He exited the bus from the open back and found Asif waiting for him.

'Where's Benny?' he asked.

'He's gonna follow us in a minute,' Charlie lied. 'Follow me,' he said and he led Asif to the Secret Garden.

As Charlie sleepily shivered towards dawn in the Secret Garden, Mr Chadwick was lacing his trainers for an early morning run around the beautiful grounds. 'It's good for the soul,' he would say. And you can imagine his surprise when, approaching the first XI cricket pitch, he looked up to see a big old red London Routemaster parked neatly over the square.

He entered to investigate and looked around for clues on the ground floor but found only an empty bottle of vodka. He gained the upper deck and saw the torso of somebody lying across the back row of seats. As he made his way to the back of the bus, that maniacal grin lit up his bitter face as he recognised the unconscious boy at the back of the bus. He shook him roughly awake and as comprehension seeped into Benny's bleary eyes, Chadwick gazed down at him and whispered happily, 'Bye bye, Benjamin.'

Charlie had to act fast. He was sure that he had got Benny expelled and possibly worse but he now had to follow through on his cowardice and save his own skin. They would know that Benny hadn't acted alone but they couldn't prove it. And Benny wouldn't tell. He didn't betray his friends. Still, they would suspect Charlie's involvement.

He glanced at his watch and saw that it was almost seven o'clock. They would have found both Benny and the bus by now, so he had to get a move on. He phoned home and was grateful when his mother answered the phone.

'Mum, it's Charlie,' he said.

'Where are you?' she demanded. 'Why didn't you come home last night?' And then in a softer voice, 'Are you okay?'

'Mum, listen I'm fine. And I did come home last night. Or at least that's what you have to tell the school if they phone.'

'What happened? What did you do?'

'Nothing,' he lied. 'It was Benny. I refused to go along with it but you know how it is. Guilt by association.'

'What did "Benny" do?' she asked. He could hear the inverted commas and he resented them.

'He stole a bus.'

There was a pause on the other end of the line before her exasperated voice groaned, 'Oh, Charlie.'

'You have to tell them that I slept at home, Mum,' Charlie begged. 'They'll expel me. Or worse.'

'I won't lie for you, Charlie.' But he knew that she would.

'I have to go, Mum. I'll be in touch soon.'

She started to speak but he hung up. Now he had to get rid of Asif. He shook him roughly awake.

'You've gotta get outta here, man.'

Asif blinked and looked around. 'Where's Benny?' he asked.

'He's fine,' Charlie lied and proceeded to tell him the route through the woods to the town of Downsouth where he could catch a train back to London.

'Last night was jokes, man,' Asif said. 'I can't believe we nicked a bus! That's got to be the craziest thing I've ever done. You boys are jokers!' he grinned.

Charlie didn't have time for niceties. 'Go,' he urged. 'Or we'll get busted.'

'What are you gonna do?'

'I'm gonna wait out the day here until I'm supposed to be back and then I'm gonna go to chapel and pretend nothing's happened.'

Realisation dawned on Asif. 'You left Benny there, didn't you? To take the blame?'

Charlie avoided eye contact. 'Of course not. Benny's fine. GO!' he urged once more. Asif made to speak but knew that he would be speaking to a lost cause. He shook his head and began to make his way through the undergrowth, past the remains of Benny and Sally's last supper.

Charlie had with him an almost full packet of cigarettes and he steadily chain smoked and tried hard not to think of his betrayal. He spent hours trying to justify his actions, to leave potential consequences undeveloped. But life didn't let him and at about midday he started with a fright on hearing rustling in the bushes.

'Be a deer,' he prayed as he got up from the bench and began to edge towards the escape route. 'Or a suicide squirrel.' But it was neither.

Sally Chadwick burst through the bushes, crying wildly and furiously punching Charlie. She wailed as the blows rained down. 'You fucker. You fucking shithead.' Eventually, she tired herself out and collapsed against Charlie's chest.

'Why did you do it, Charlie? Why did you leave him?' she sobbed.

'He was out of it, he couldn't move,' Charlie said.

'Then you should've carried him. He'd have carried you.'

'I know,' said Charlie. 'But he's a better man.'

'You're not a man, Charlie. You're a scared little boy. But that's his life. And mine. The police came – they took him away, Charlie.'

'I'm sorry, Sally. I really am.'

'Sorry?' she shrieked. 'Do you realise what you've done? You've just destroyed both our lives. We need each other.'

'I'm sorry, Sally,' he repeated lamely as his guilt grew.

'And are you gonna take the blame as well then?'

Charlie regained the quick composure of the wrong. 'I don't see the point of both of us getting nicked.'

She shook her head at him in disbelief, as if she was seeing him for the first time. 'You're gonna let him take all the blame? They'll throw the book at him. Drink driving, vehicle theft – he might get years.'

Charlie dismissed this notion uncomfortably. 'He won't get years. He'll get a slap on the wrists. It's a kids' prank.' He actually thought she was overreacting, he lacked the empathy to see it from her point of view. 'You guys will be reunited before you know it.'

She slapped him viciously across the cheek and the sting lasted years.

When Benny left, it changed Charlie. He felt fear afresh without him. And guilt. Mainly guilt. News of the trial had reached him and he had been wrong. Not only was Benny tried as an adult but a career-crusading judge had handed him three years. It was an incredibly harsh sentence. He was serving his stretch, ironically, at Wandsworth – the Cambridge of crime and chaos.

Charlie had taken him from Sally and her from him and he knew he had broken both their hearts. Had he been jealous of their love? If so, he had successfully scuppered it. Sally hadn't the heart to carry on with Benny. She couldn't bear the idea of seeing him only at visiting hours and not in the splendour of their illicit nights. She cut contact.

Charlie had got away with everything because Benny had refused to grass and he was left to continue in the monotonous comfort of of Downsouth College. But it didn't comfort him. Survivor's guilt, I guess. His disinclination to carry Benny from that ridiculous

Routemaster to the safety of the Secret Garden was an act of cowardice. He knew that but then again, he had long known himself to be a coward and had never tried to do anything about it. And his fear and his guilt and his cowardice led to where they often do – cruelty.

Not to everyone. Not all the time. But Charlie changed. A slashing jibe, a casual threat, a look of intense, all-encompassing hate that – if only his victims understood – pointed inwards and not at their scared faces. He now shouldered Benny's demons as he felt he should – it was the decent thing to do.

They plagued him and they haunted him and they roused his recklessness. But the school just never caught him. The spliffs outside the headmaster's office, the drinking in the common room, the cigarettes walking to class, the bored terrorisation of the younger boys as he tried to share his fear around.

Thank God, Tom Leary was there. He was the only friend that Charlie had left after Benny had departed and he tempered his savagery with an odd note of caution, a gentle remonstration, sympathy for the devil. And this perhaps prevented tragedy. Or delayed it. It carried him through to the end of the school year and into the arms of a long and lonely blissful summer.

CHAPTER TEN

Horatio Smith-Jones was a prick. Far be it for me to sway your judgement, gentle reader, but trust me on this one. Horatio Smith-Jones was a monumental arsehole.

He was in Charlie's year and they clashed early on. Horatio was fond of complaining loudly about the riff-raff that contaminated Downsouth College and claimed that his father, a hugely wealthy and morally erratic businessman, held sway with the powers that be at the school.

This was probably true. He had donated a state of the art computer room to the school which coincided remarkably with his son's acceptance into the institution, despite having failed to achieve the required grades. For poor Horatio had inherited his mother's intellect – the only slight blemish on an otherwise distinguished career as an objectified plastic trophy.

So perhaps we cannot judge poor Horatio too harshly, for nurture had corrupted an innately imbecilic nature to produce, as I have intimated, a devious, greedy, arrogant, ignorant, narcissistic prick.

So it was a surprise to Charlie therefore when one crisp February morning, about a year after Benny's expulsion, as he walked through the woods to one of his private smoking holes that he came across Horatio with his trousers around his ankles.

Charlie was promptly told to fuck off but not before he had caught sight of the girl on her knees. He did not begrudge her for not saying hello, for Sally Chadwick had been well trained in manners and knew better than to speak with her mouth full.

Charlie left them to it.

A few days after this traumatic event, Charlie was sitting alone in the Secret Garden, when he started at the sound of rustling in the bushes. Sally Chadwick entered, looking bashful but determined.

Charlie laughed at her. 'Horatio Smith-Jones?' he snarled, savouring the distaste of the name.

She reached him and crossed her arms defiantly.

'Horatio Smith-Jones,' he said, shaking his head and tutting as a disappointed parent might at a naughty child. 'That's quite a change from Benny,' he said. 'And a toyboy too. He's in my year.' Charlie scoffed.

'I don't fucking care what you think, Charlie,' she said.

'Which would explain why you're here,' he retorted.

'He looks after me.'

'You don't have to explain yourself to me.'

'He takes me to nice restaurants.'

'In exchange for blowjobs in the woods?'

'Fuck off, Charlie,' she said. 'It's your fault that Benny's gone. If it wasn't for you, none of this would have happened. So I don't know where you get the fucking cheek to have a go at me about who I go out with. It's none of your business.'

Charlie accepted this. 'I know, Sally. But *Horatio Smith-Jones? Seriously?* Is there no one else who is slightly more…' he searched for the word and knew he still hadn't found it when he said, 'nice?'

'You don't know him, Charlie.'

'I know him well enough. I know that he's a million miles away from Benny.'

'But Benny's gone,' she reminded him. 'He's a million miles away from me. And I can't wait around forever.'

The truth was she needed to have someone looking out for her and she thought that Horatio, with his endless gifts, was doing that.

'I just don't want to see you getting hurt, that's all.'

'You didn't think too much about that when you left Benny in that bus.'

'Are you ever going to forgive me for that?' Charlie asked.

'No.'

'Fair enough. But if you're trying to punish me by going out with Horatio, then that is fucking stupid.'

'What do you mean "punish you",' her voice rose in octave and volume. 'This has nothing to do with you. You're so fucking self-centred, Charlie.'

They both seemed to realise simultaneously that they were starting a fight that neither had the heart for. It was too big. And they needed each other in a strange, indefinable way. It had to do with Benny.

'I'm sorry.'

'No, I'm sorry.'

'Truce?'

'Truce.'

They hugged and she sat down next to him and they spent the afternoon chatting and carefully skirting around any potentially incendiary topics. When she left, Charlie had a strange urge to cry. He never questioned his feelings towards Sally. Not once. But it is true to say that he had been totally enraptured by the times he had spent with her and Benny together and he was maybe a little jealous of the bond that they shared.

The worst news Charlie received that spring was that Tom Leary was leaving Downsouth. He was his last remaining friend and had been an incredible source of comfort and support. He was gutted.

'How come?' he asked when Tom told him.

'Combination of things,' Tom said. 'My parents are really struggling to pay the fees for one thing.'

'What about your scholarship?'

'Even with that, man, they just don't have the cash.'

'Can't you apply for a bursary or something?'

'Maybe. But I'm done with this place, man. I turned sixteen last week and they still treat me like a ten-year-old. It ain't worth the hassle. I've got a place at a sixth form college. No uniform, no hymn singing, normal people, it sounds pretty good.'

'It does,' Charlie admitted. 'But don't go,' he pleaded.

Tom laughed. 'Why don't you leave too? You fucking hate this place.'

Why indeed? 'I dunno man. All my fees are paid for and I guess I'm just resigned to the fact. It's only two more years. Plus, I reckon my Dad would call me a "quitter" if I left.'

'Why don't you ask your folks? I bet they'd say yes.'

'Yeah, maybe I will.' But he knew he wouldn't. It was as if he felt that Downsouth was his rightful punishment. Or maybe it was Stockholm syndrome. Then again, maybe not. Maybe he just didn't want the RSPB to get the rest of his school fees.

CHAPTER ELEVEN

When he returned to school in September, he felt truly alone. Tom Leary was gone and Charlie felt his loss acutely. Without him, Charlie's manic side was utterly unleashed. He just didn't care about anything any more. He was in constant trouble and although it troubled him, he didn't stop. He couldn't. He simply couldn't do his homework and he definitely couldn't resist answering back to teachers. He couldn't wear his uniform properly and he couldn't shine his shoes. He couldn't quit smoking and he couldn't stop being mean to people. He couldn't bear his solitude and he couldn't tolerate company. With one possible exception. Sally. She would come, on occasion, and find him in the Secret Garden and they would chat, once more skirting around any inflammatory issues. She became quite worried about him and he craved her concern.

'To be honest, it's an almighty struggle to get out of bed in the morning.'

'Oh, Charlie, is there anything I can do?'

'No it's not your fault. I just can't seem to get out of this rut.'

'Dad was talking about you the other day.'

'Yeah?'

'Yeah. He said you're heading for expulsion.'

Charlie really didn't care. There was a pause and Charlie changed the subject. He broke their unspoken rule.

'So how's it going with you and Horatio?' Her eyes flashed him a warning. 'I'm just asking,' he said.

'It's good thanks…' She paused. 'It's not like with Benny though.'

Charlie triumphed as trumpets blasted through his body. He retained a poker face. 'But he's looking after you?'

'Yes. He's very good to me. And Dad knows now and he loves him because he's on the rugby team.'

'Well, I hope it all goes well for you.' Sally gave him a sceptical expression. 'I'm serious.' He wasn't.

'Thank you, Charlie, that means a lot to me.'

Charlie was clinging on at Downsouth. He had begun to see quite a lot of the headmaster's office. He had first been called in for a 'chat' about a month before his exams.

'Soooooooooooooo,' the headmaster had said. 'Mr Dixon.'

'Yes, sir?'

'What's wrong?'

'Sorry, sir?'

'All this bad behaviour, these endless detentions, being caught smoking. What's the matter?'

'Nothing, sir.'

'Well, it certainly doesn't look like nothing,' he said. 'Your teachers are not predicting you very good grades for your AS levels.'

'They're wrong, sir.'

'Is that so?'

'Yes, sir.'

'Nonetheless, I called you here to give you fair warning. I'm a very fair man, Dixon, a very reasonable man, a very just man, Dixon. I'm a very kind-hearted man Dixon. I care deeply about my students, Dixon. I care for their emotional well-being and not just their academic prowess. Nonetheless, we can't have one bad set of grades affecting our position in the league table. It wouldn't be fair, Dixon, or just or reasonable. You understand?'

'You're expelling me?'

'Oh lord, no,' chortled the headmaster. 'I'm asking you to sit the exams as an external candidate. Well, actually I'm telling you. We'll think about whether you should come back for your final year when the grades are published in the summer.'

'Thank you, sir.'

'As I told you, Dixon, I'm a very fair man.'

'Yes you are, sir. Is there anything else, sir?'

'No, that will be all, Dixon.'

'Sir.'

He was walking back to his boarding house when he saw Horatio Smith-Jones approaching him. He silently handed Charlie an envelope.

'What's this?' Charlie asked as he tore at it.

'An invite to my eighteenth.' Horatio smiled sarcastically, 'I'd be really honoured if you would come.'

'Sally's idea?' Charlie asked.

'Yep, for some strange reason she wants you there but let me be very clear that I don't.' Charlie resolved there and then to make an appearance.

'Yeah, well I think I'm busy that day anyway,' said Charlie looking at the invite. 'July 6th, yeah. I'm watching paint dry I think.'

Horatio pulled a face at him. 'Do you ever wonder why you don't have any friends?' he asked.

Charlie desperately tried to believe that the comment didn't hurt. 'No, I don't think about it too often to be honest. Though if I did, I suppose I'd conclude that if being "popular" meant being like you, I'd rather toss myself off using sandpaper for lube.'

Horatio shook his head in disbelief. 'You're such a fuck up. Why does Sally like you? I just don't get it.'

'Who knows? She must be a terrible judge of character. Her choice of boyfriend for example…'

'Watch it, Dixon,' his neck tightened. 'Don't give me an excuse to floor you.'

'Violence, Horatio? How big and clever you are.'

'Fuck off, Dixon. I've done what Sally asked me to, I've given you the damn invite. Just do me a favour and don't turn up, okay?'

'It'd be a pleasure,' said Charlie and he walked away.

The last few weeks of term went fantastically slowly. But Charlie now had an extreme motivation. For some obscure reason, to Charlie's skewered brain, sitting his exams as an independent candidate greatly appealed to him and for the first time in his life he actually worked hard. Really hard. Even the teachers noticed, and the Damocles sword of expulsion seemed to withdraw.

He was supremely confident on sitting his exams (as an independent) that he had nailed every one and would be able to return to Downsouth the following year and complete his sentence. But first of all, there were the summer holidays and they were his. They belonged to him and he was greatly looking forward to them.

He hadn't really thought about Horatio's party but on the Tuesday following the end of term, he got a call from Sally.

'Hey,' he said, picking up. 'How are you?'

'Good, thanks, we're getting ready for the party. You're coming right?'

'Erm, well, er, um.'

'Come,' she said. 'I didn't get a chance to see you before you left.'

83

'Erm, well, er, um.' He had already decided to go but he just wanted to hear Sally say how much it would mean to her, how it would make her day, how it wouldn't be the same without him…

'Well, it's up to you,' she said.

'I'll be there,' he said.

'Awesome, well, I've got to run now. See you tomorrow.'

'See you tomorrow.'

Beep beep beep.

The Smith-Jones' mansion was in the countryside north of London. He got a train from King's Cross and then a taxi from the station. There were other people from his year at Downsouth on the train and at the station but nobody said a word to him. When he arrived at the obscene house, his cabbie said to him, 'Fucking hell, this place is a bit posh,' and Charlie laughed and agreed and paid him.

He accepted a glass of champagne from one of the waitresses and stood around on his own, grabbing canapés as they went by and signalling for constant refills of champagne. He was determined to get his money's worth.

A woman walked towards him and it took him a moment to realise it was Sally. She looked utterly gorgeous. She wore a long, sleeveless dress with a plunging neckline that exposed her ample cleavage, pert and youthful and harbouring a Tiffany heart. Her skin was opulent, her eyes shining, her teeth dazzling as she smiled.

'You came,' she said and kissed him on the cheek.

'I came,' said Charlie. 'Sally. You look…erm… absolutely unbelievable.'

'Are you coming on to me, Charlie?' she teased.

'As if,' he said. 'So where's the birthday boy?' The

question was answered as Horatio came up beside Sally, put his arm around her and kissed her neck. She giggled. Charlie's stomach churned.

'You came,' he said to Charlie in a very different tone to Sally.

'I came,' he said again.

Horatio affected the gracious host and, in fairness to him, he achieved it magnanimously. 'Well, you're very welcome,' he slicked. 'Help yourself to anything you want.' He turned to Sally. 'Sweetheart, can I have a word with you for a minute?'

'Excuse us,' she said and followed Horatio across the room. Charlie stared after them. They were adults, he realised. And he thought disquietingly that he had perhaps misjudged Horatio and that he seemed to make Sally happy. Perhaps, this is what he had been invited to be shown.

He went to the bar and found himself a seat and settled in. A couple of generous souls came to chat to him but Sally was nowhere to be seen. He kept on devouring champagne and canapés and when the champagne began to make urgent appeals to his bladder, he tried to stand up. Attempting this, he became fully aware of just how drunk he was as he swayed unsteadily for a moment before slumping back into his seat. He steadied himself and tried again and this time he succeeded, although it took an almighty effort.

Charlie staggered through a sea of people who he disliked and who disliked him. The boys aggressively stood their ground, sticking out shoulders as he passed while the girls sucked in their skeletally thin bodies to be sure of avoiding all contamination.

On the first floor there was a queue for both bathrooms

and so he stumbled up the next flight of steps to try his luck there. The first three doors were dark, empty bedrooms. The fourth was also a bedroom but the light was on. Two half-naked bodies, wrestling on the bed, turned their heads as the door opened and Charlie swayed in the frame.

Through his drunkenness he clearly recognised the boy as Horatio Smith-Jones and the girl dimly as definitely not being Sally Chadwick. He pointed an accusing finger at Horatio and slurred, 'YoubastardcheatSallypoorSallybastard.' Horatio Smith-Jones calmly stood up and, walking over to Charlie, grabbed him by the neck.

'You fucking mention a word of this to Sally and I'll kill you,' he said. Charlie protested hoarsely but, lacking oxygen, he quickly acquiesced and Horatio relinquished his grip. Charlie knew he couldn't face people, least of all Sally. And he felt sleepy and boozy and remembering the bedrooms on the floor, he entered one and slumped on to the bed with the intention of having nothing more than a brief lie-down.

'Eurgh, that's minging – he's pissed himself,' a high voice shrieked.

Charlie returned to consciousness.

He opened his eyes and groaned as he saw the thirty faces that were crowded into the room looking down on him. Some were marked with disgust, others with delight and all were extremely hostile. He saw Sally standing by the door but she shook her head, pursed her lips and fled the room.

Somebody punched him hard in the stomach, winding him and he nearly puked. Horatio Smith-Jones leaned down over him, smiled unpleasantly and said, 'I think you've outstayed your welcome now, Dixon.'

He dragged him up off the bed and Charlie felt himself pushed and shoved through the house, down the stairs, past mocking eyes and hurled out of the front door. He cut his hand on the gravel as he tried to break his fall and he didn't have the will to get up. He felt an intense pressure bubble through him, let out an anguished cry and wept.

Some time passed before Charlie had finally exhausted his tear ducts, but when he did he morosely dragged himself to his feet and determined to get far, far away from the house and its revellers. Becoming lost twice, it took him the best part of an hour to walk to the train station and, when he finally arrived, sunrise was not far away. Still, the commuter trains had not yet started running and Charlie lay down on a bench and fell asleep.

Unbeknownst to him, during his first vulnerable slumber that night, his eyebrows had been shaved off and had been drawn in, comically raised, in permanent marker. He also had an inky penis on his left cheek that had been partially smudged by his tears.

He was shaken awake by a railway worker who looked at him with distant sympathy. 'You okay, son?' he asked. Charlie nodded. 'You can't sleep here,' the man said. 'Have you got a ticket to travel?' Charlie nodded and pulled out his overnight return.

'Okay, son, train to London will be here in a minute. You had a rough night?'

'Something like that,' he said.

When he reached London, he didn't know what bus to take to get back to Wandsworth and so he decided to get the tube to somewhere he did know was on his bus route. The underground platform was heaving with commuters. He walked further down to where the crowd seemed thinner. Most people, utterly engaged with pretending there were no other people sharing their commute, kept their eyes firmly on their reading materials but the few people who did catch his eye, grinned at him. He stopped by a pregnant lady, who glanced up at him and then did a cartoonish double take to look at him again. She was pretty. Not a young mother, but radiant in her pregnancy.

She gave him a sympathetic smile which confused him until the train pulled up and as it flashed by he saw a reflection of himself and his strange appearance. His hands moved up to rub his absent eyebrows in disbelief. Gone. He felt slightly violated and quite annoyed and he wanted more than anything to get home and go to bed. The hangover depressed him as much as the memory of the previous night but as the train slowed to a stop, he saw that the carriage was packed and only one person got off. He was about to jump in but the pregnant lady caught his eye again and reluctantly he smiled and motioned for her to get on.

There might have been space for Charlie too but for a man with a huge backpack. As the doors closed, the man looked up and Charlie thought he recognised him. As if! What are the chances? Charlie waved animatedly but those eyes had died and they looked straight through him. And the train was gone.

After being evacuated from the tube network and wandering south in the daze of his hangover, Charlie learned what had happened although the reports were patchy at first. Nonetheless, it was clear. London had been attacked. Charlie was quite upset. He asked, like Yossarian did, why are they trying to kill me?

In the days and weeks that followed, Charlie refused

to read the newspapers or look at the faces of either murderers or victims. He was plagued by the thought that the man he had believed to be Asif with the big backpack would be a photo in the paper. And that the pretty pregnant lady would also appear. He knew it was unlikely that it had been that train or that man but he didn't want to know. It would bring history far too close to him. And most of all, he thought about his kind courtesy in letting the pregnant lady on to the train. Did he in fact motion two lives to their deaths?

The rest of that summer was lonely. He went on holiday with his parents to Italy but, really, two months passed him by without him doing a single tangible thing. Most days he would go to Wandsworth Common and spend the day getting stoned. When his results came through, and they were good, the headmaster wrote to invite him back for his final year. He was a very decent man. In a very strange way, he was almost looking forward to returning for his last year at Downsouth College. It felt like the end was nearing and the sooner it was over, then perhaps life would actually start for real.

CHAPTER TWELVE

The school year dragged slowly by. The teachers were trying to pressure him to work hard but he had got an easy offer from Upnorth University and he planned to do just what he needed to meet its requirements. Nothing more.

He spent much of his time alone in the woods, smoking and reading junk. And feeling sorry for himself. He had always felt sorry for himself.

He hadn't heard from Sally since the party the previous summer and he didn't expect to. She was presumably still with Horatio Smith-Jones, who continued to strut around school with the unearned entitlement of the rich and to take hearty pleasure in recounting to absolutely anybody the story of Charlie's humiliation at his party. There can't have been a single person in the school, teachers included, who didn't know that he had pissed himself and had his eyebrows shaved off that summer.

Valentine's Day had again come round and he was spending the afternoon alone in the Secret Garden when he heard rustling in the bushes and had the certain intuition that it was Sally Chadwick. It was. She sat down silently beside him and fumbled in the pocket of her gilet from where she withdrew a spliff.

'Twos this with me?'

He nodded and she lit it, inhaling a long needy drag. She passed the joint to Charlie and he too inhaled a long needy drag. He passed it back.

'So how are you?' he said.

'Okay, I guess.' She was definitely here to tell him something but was not ready to disclose what just yet. She looked around and her gaze lingered on the bushes where, three years on, the gas stove from her last supper with Benny could still just be seen.

She toked again, returned the spliff to Charlie and stood up. She paced aimlessly around in a tight circle until she came face to face with Charlie.

'I'm sorry for what they did to you at the party,' she said.

Charlie shrugged. 'I'm sorry for embarrassing you,' he ventured to return.

'You managed to get home in the end?'

'Yeah, eventually, but I got somewhat caught up in the whole terrorist attacks thing.'

'I tried to call to check you were okay but all the networks were jammed.'

'I wasn't expecting you to call.'

This definitely wasn't what she had come here to say. The spliff passed between them in silence for a while.

Finally she said, 'Benny came to see me last week.'

'He's out?' Excitement and fear penetrated his haze.

'Yeah, he's out.'

'How is he?'

'Angry,' she said. Charlie looked nervous and she added, 'But not with you in particular. With the whole fucking world. He's changed. There's no humour in his eyes any more. Just cruelty and anger. I don't know what happened to him in jail but it's not the Benny I know.'

'What did he say?'

'He gave a brief account of his time and said that things had happened to him but he refused to say what. He sounded bitter and angry but he said that none of it would matter if we got back together. He said he had thought about me every day.' Here, she began to sob and sat back down on the bench, leaning in to Charlie for comfort.

'What did you say?'

'I told him I was with Horatio now. That I'd had to move on.' She sobbed again.

Charlie's heart sank. He had always hoped that somehow his crime would be erased if, in the end, Benny and Sally were reunited as he truly believed they were supposed to be.

'How did he react?'

'He cried, Charlie. I've never seen him cry. And then eventually his tears stopped and his face hardened. He looked at me with real hatred and said, 'Well, I don't fucking need you anyway – you abandoned me like everybody else." And he just left.'

Charlie, not believing what he was saying in the least, said, 'Well, maybe it's for the best. Like you said, you're with Horatio now.'

She sobbed harder.

'What's the matter?' he said.

'Horatio dumped me last night. By text. On the day before Valentine's. He's been fucking some other girl for almost a year.'

As Charlie drew her in to comfort her, his heart was pounding with rage at Horatio, at the world, at the cruelty of life but, most of all, at himself. For he knew that this suffering, that this pain and anguish, that the ugly spectacle of unfulfilled love and broken hearts all came back to his cowardice, his betrayal of Benny, his capacity for fear.

Every time he saw Horatio over the following months he wanted to punch the smug grin off his face. But of course he didn't. He pretended to himself that this was out of a high-minded dislike of violence. More accurately, it was because Horatio would beat him black and blue.

Reading the paper one day, he was convinced that Horatio's smugness would now evaporate. Charlie read with delight how his father, amongst others, had donated one million pounds to the political party in power, angling for a lordship. Lord Smith-Jones of Corruptionshire. Scum.

But, if anything, the smugness of Horatio increased and nobody at Downsouth seemed to think that this was scandalous. 'Old Smith-Jones, eh? What's he like, the cheeky chap? Trying to buy a lordship! Well, I suppose he can do what he likes with his money.'

Charlie was counting down the days until he could finally leave this astonishingly backward place. His A levels were fast approaching and he approached them with the breezy confidence of the unambitious, taking his revision with him to the woods.

The exams were fine, albeit a boring waste of time. Charlie left each one feeling confident that he had done the necessary to get to Upnorth. During the last one, however, he was unbelievably itchy to finish. He saw that three hours stood between him and the end of Downsouth and he could barely contain himself. He hurriedly scribbled a few essays and left early. And that was it. It was over. As he left the examination hall and stepped into the beautiful sunshine of a June afternoon, he extended his arms to the world, leant back his head and exploded with a howl of happiness. A teacher rushed out of the examination hall to chastise him but he ignored him and walked in the direction of the woods.

His happiness was soon replaced with anger, however, for as he was walking past the headmaster's office he saw a bright red Italian sports car with the licence plate 'RSJ 1' – the vehicle of 'Lord' Smith-Jones. Supercilious bastard, he thought.

He wanted revenge upon the last five years and on the place and the environment that had inflicted them. A more suitable target might have been Charlie himself, for the horrors of the last five years were in no small part due to his own failures of imagination and courage. But he had spent enough time tormenting himself for his failures and decided it was time to pick on someone else.

So when Charlie saw the gleaming red Ferrari parked outside the headmaster's office, he decided that it was time to take action. For himself or for justice or for Sally or for them all, it is hard to say, but Benny, as ever, urged him on. He went to the tool sheds, behind which he sometimes smoked, and crashed his shoulder against the door. It hurt like hell but the door opened. Almost immediately he found what he was looking for. He grabbed a tin of white paint and a brush and left quickly.

He made his way to near where the car was parked and hid behind a helpful bush. He waited for some figures to pass and then when the coast was clear, he sprang into action. He rushed towards the car, plonked the tin of paint on the ridiculously low bonnet, opened it and submerged the brush. He only needed to submerge the brush twice to daub the windshield with seven appropriate characters:

C 4 H
SCUM

With this quickly achieved he tipped the tin of paint over and let it run over the bonnet before running to the safety of the woods where he threw the brush into the undergrowth. Exhilarated, he went to the Secret Garden and lit a spliff that he had been saving for after his final exam. But there had been a witness to his crime.

Sally Chadwick had been watching out of a window of her father's house and had seen him do it. She followed him into the woods and rushed towards the Secret Garden, where she ran towards him as he stood up, threw her arms around his neck and gave him a full blown smacker on the lips.

'Thank you,' she said, smiling and affectionately ruffling his hair.

'Thank *you*,' he replied, referring to the kiss. 'Smoke?' he offered and together they spent the afternoon basking in the sunshine of the Secret Garden, laughing at the imagined face of 'Lord' Smith-Jones and smoking and forgetting, for a while, the sorrows of the past.

As the sky darkened, he and Sally parted. There was a knowing finality to it. Their lives would now go separate ways. He apologised once more for leaving Benny in the bus and she took his hands and forgave him.

'I understand,' she said. 'It's not easy, this life we lead. We all make mistakes. But keep trying, Charlie.'

'I will,' he promised and, after saying goodbye, he walked down to Downsouth station, leaving her to an uncertain future that she didn't deserve.

The jubilation of leaving Downsouth lasted all summer long and he was proud of himself for making it through those five years. Although Charlie had made it harder for himself than it needed to be, I beg you, gentle reader, to excuse him a little in light of his tender years and his amazing propensity for cowardice.

In the middle of August the confirmation came that he

had attained the necessary grades to attend Upnorth University and he arrived shortly after his eighteenth birthday, confident that life was about to change for the better.

PART TWO

CHAPTER ONE

I'm not inclined to dwell too much on the reliability of the narrative of Charlie's early years for I was not there. But this bit I know about. This is when, with distant sympathy, I began to watch and write about the fall of Charlie Dixon.

I had just been through Fresher's Week when we met. And quite a week it was. Other than excessive amounts of alcohol, it was significant for a couple of reasons. I tried hard drugs for the first time. They were fun.

I also didn't make a single friend. It's not that I was alone during this week but the people who I was partying with, I was doing so not out of the first buds of friendship but out of the convenience of the coincidence of being in the same halls as them. And fuck me, it was boring at times. The small talk for example:

'Hi.'
'Hi.'
'What's your name?'
'What's your name?'
'What halls are you in?'
'What halls are you in?'
'What course are you doing?'
'What course are you doing?'
'Where do you come from?'
'Where do you come from?'
'Did you take a gap year?'
'Did you take a gap year?'
'What school were you at?'

'What school were you at?'
'Ohh! Do you know blah blah?'
'No.'

Anyway, I resisted the temptation of having a t-shirt printed with all these answers on it and patiently repeated this conversation with perhaps one hundred people over the course of the week.

When my first seminar came around the following week, I was actually pretty glad. I can't quite remember the name of the class but I believe it was called something like 'How to slag off incredible writers and thus embrace the spiteful world of academia'. Something like that anyway.

When we were all seated in a learning-environment-enhancing semicircle, the tutor introduced himself. I wish he hadn't bothered. He was a paradigm of eccentricity for its own sake and Oh, isn't it quirky? Isn't it charming? No. Yawn.

He told us to close our eyes and put our hands on our laps with our palms facing the ceiling and sit there in silence for a minute and 'give ourselves permission to be here and let our energy descend upon this room'. With my eyes wide open I saw the boy opposite me stifling an urge to giggle.

When we had given ourselves permission to be there, the lecherer swung his goggly eyes around the room, smiling, nodding and panting like one of those little dogs people put in their cars.

'Soooooooooooooooooooo,' he said. 'Simple task. I would like you all to introduce yourselves and tell me the name of your favourite book.'

He motioned for the boy, who I had seen suppressing

giggles at the other end of the semicircle, to begin. The boy looked at his feet and muttered, 'I'm Charlie Dixon and my favourite book is…err…Lucky Jim.' His front tooth bit his lower lip as he glanced up at the lecherer who was giving him a look of studied disappointment.

I, however, was giving him a look of intense interest. It was also my favourite book, you see. We went round the semi-circle.

'War and Peeeeeeeace.'

'Pride and Prejudeeeeeeeeeeeeece.'

These came from two very confident girls and were greeted with enthusiastic nods and exhalations from the lecherer. Whether this was about the choice of books or their instinctively academic tendency to elongate their words was hard to say because, to me, it seemed that the lecherer was being enthusiastic about their tits, which were the object of his gaze.

Finally it came to me and I surrendered my name and repeated Charlie Dixon's answer. Charlie looked up at me and we gave each other a little nod of complicity or respect. Or chauvinistic solidarity.

The rest of the seminar was incredibly tedious. When it was over, I approached Charlie in the corridor.

'Charlie, isn't it?' I said.

'Yeah, mate, and you're my book buddy!' he replied with a smile.

'Fancy a pint?' we asked at the same time.

It was eleven in the morning and the student bar was packed. I never failed to find this amusing. We grabbed a couple of pints and settled out on the terrace, the early autumn sunshine had not yet subsided. It was the first opening conversation I had with somebody at university that didn't follow the same tedious outline of the others.

Naturally, we talked about our joint passion for Lucky Jim. I couldn't get over his name. 'Dixon'. Un-fucking-believable. We had both studied it for A level and therefore had exactly the same ideas about the book – the ideas that the exam board had dictated we should have. But then, after a few pints, Charlie came up with an idea that I hadn't thought about and it became the maxim of our friendship, and the cornerstone of our ambitions. At least for a while.

'I just love that bit at the end when he's pissed and giving the lecture and it says something like, "He resolved to do some good, however little, for some present, however few." When I read that, I thought "bang on", that's what it's all about, innit? We might not be able to change the world but, you know, even if we just do the best we can to brighten up a few people's lives then we've done okay.'

I liked that. I liked that a lot. The practical question of how to do some good while at Upnorth remained elusive but that motto dictated our thoughts about the future. We said we would go to Africa together and do charity work or something. I was looking forward to that.

That first year of Upnorth was one of the happiest of my life and I think I can say the same for Charlie Dixon. He was my first best friend and, for that first year at least, I had him mainly to myself. I don't really know why I liked him so much – it was just one of those chemical things. Did I love him? Yeah, I think I probably did. Why am I writing his fall? I don't want to dwell on it.

Anyway, we were inseparable that year and he told me all about his past. About his Gran and about Downsouth and Benny and Sally and I found it fascinating. It was certainly more interesting than my school days. We sat together in the lectures we shared and even in some that we didn't. We spent many hours in the pub but even

102

more in either one of our rooms getting stoned. For it was a very hazy year and I'm not sure there was a day that we didn't smoke.

We went out from time to time, took pills and tried to pull girls. We were never very successful though. For my part, I don't think my heart was really in it. Charlie pulled once or twice but they were never more than one night stands.

In fact, by this point in his life, Charlie had never slept with anybody twice. I don't know what it was. He was attracted by the idea of sex and it wasn't out of deliberate cruelty that he never called them again but he just didn't see that as part of the contract. His self-esteem wasn't exactly overflowing and he figured, without resentment, that they didn't want him to call. In this he sold them short. And himself. Or maybe he had just never felt love. Affection and attraction, perhaps. But not love.

When the time came to look for accommodation for our second year, we naturally looked together. The first place we found was a very reasonably priced two-bedroom flat overlooking the mosque and an hour later we signed the contract. I was ecstatic.

I moved into our house at the start of the lease in July and spent my entire summer in Upnorth. It was damn boring. I worked in a bar at nights and spent my days trying to write. After a while I gave up on this because every word I set down on the page smelt funny.

Charlie came up a couple of weeks before the start of term having enjoyed a happy summer and seemed determined to approach life with renewed vigour. He talked of quitting pot and stopping all the fucking about of Fresher's Year. He would work hard and get good grades. He would join societies and do extracurricular activities.

Luckily, this was a plan for when term started and in the couple of weeks before then he was happy to resume the *mode de vie* of first year. Thus, we bought an ounce of hydroponic super skunk and spent ten days in a happy haze.

Following through on his alleged new resolve, Charlie arose one morning and asked me if I wanted to go to the Fresher's Fair with him. I declined, having a deep aversion for anything resembling team spirit or extracurricular activities. Instead, I lit a spliff as he walked out the door.

The fair was in the vast sports hall of the university and there were brightly coloured stalls trying to entice new members to various societies. Charlie must have got a bit over-excited because as he passed Yoga, Boxing, Football, Mountaineering, Tae-Kwan-do, Ultimate Frisbee and even Trampolining, he signed up for them all. He would never attend a single one.

He wandered through the hall and passed the societies for the three main political parties of the country. They were the blandest stalls of them all and it was hard to distinguish between them – they were set up so close together and the people around them all looked and dressed the same.

He passed these by to find himself by the next stall, erected some distance apart. A vast Union Jack hung behind the stall around which various misfits were talking angrily to intimidated Freshers. Distaste naturally assaulted Charlie's senses and he had started to walk away when somebody shouted his name.

He couldn't believe it. It was Benny. Benny jogged towards him and Charlie was half-expecting violence, but he was forever misjudging Benny.

'Charlie, my boy,' he exclaimed as he slapped him on the back.

'Benny, listen. I'm so sorry about the whole bus thing. I…' but Benny cut him off.

'Ancient history, mate, don't worry about it.'

He was wearing a white vest, there was a Union Jack tattooed on a bulging bicep and the hair was cropped. How do you describe a stereotype without stereotyping them?

'So what are you doing here?' Benny asked Charlie.

'Uni,' he answered densely, 'Yourself?'

'Same, bruv. What year are you in?'

'Second.'

'Me too. Strange that we haven't seen each other before now. What are you studying?'

'English,' Charlie replied.

'Naturally. I would've done the same but didn't get the grades. Blagged my way through clearing, doing sociology, innit?'

Well, it's good that a sociopath should at least be informed.

Charlie asked tentatively, 'So what happened after, you know, the whole bus thing?'

'I was expelled. Then I got sent down to Wandsworth for a bit. Sally abandoned me. Then I got out.' His manner was breezy but his voice was hard and dark. He saw Charlie's apprehension and added, 'But don't worry about it, mate, ancient history as I said. Still, got my A levels done eventually and here we both are. Together again and in the same year!'

Charlie hadn't counted on this. When he left Benny in the bus that night, he was somewhat banking on never seeing him again. But here he was. And a racist revolutionary no less. Obviously.

'So what's all this about?' asked Charlie indicating the huge Union Jack.

Benny looked shifty but Charlie didn't notice – he just took him at his word. 'We're called the Defence of the Realm League. It's an organisation we've set up to encourage the promotion of British values and to facilitate the integration of immigrants.'

'Oh, wow,' Charlie said. 'That sounds interesting. I was half-fearing that it had something to do with Chadwick, what with all the Union Jacks!'

Benny did not even smile, for of course the name evoked Sally too. 'No,' he said tersely. 'We're trying to unite all the people in Britain under one flag, and one set of values.'

'Cool,' said Charlie. 'Sounds like an interesting organisation.'

Benny paused for a moment, trying to work out whether Charlie was playing with him or was as ingenuously idiotic as he seemed. 'We're having a party tonight for all the new members, if you fancy coming?'

Charlie smiled, nodding. 'I'd love to, mate – it has been far too long since I've had a beer with Benny Stone. I can't believe we've bumped into each other again.'

'Yeah,' said Benny. 'Crazy, huh?'

Charlie nodded. They swapped numbers and Benny told him the time and location of the party before excusing himself.

'Anyway, man, I've got to get back to recruiting for the cause but let's catch up properly this evening.'

'Cool, man, in a bit.'

'In a bit.'

I remember very clearly when Charlie returned from

the Fresher's Fair, despite being pretty baked by then. He came into the sitting-room and I passed him the joint I had just lit. He sat down opposite me and I turned off the TV, which had been informing me about the run on Upnorth Bank.

'Easy, bruv,' I croaked. 'How was the fair?'

'Yeah, really good,' he enthused, being still capable of enthusiasm after only one toke.

'Sign up for anything?'

'Yeah, loads, mate. But the craziest thing happened. You know the guy I told you about from Downsouth who I nicked a bus with?'

'Benny?' I said. I've got a good memory.

'Yeah, that's the one. Well, he's here at Upnorth and I bumped in to him at the fair.'

'I wouldn't think he was too happy to see you.'

'Nah, bruv, he was cool. Said it was all ancient history and he invited me to a party tonight. You wanna come?'

'Sure, mate, why not?'

CHAPTER TWO

A dingy social club was the venue. Dank, musty and stale it was. It was vibrant in an anarchic sense but it lacked true romance, for the men here were not heroes – they were just loud and hateful drunks. We made our way to the bar through a sea of skinheads and bought two pints of flat lager. Charlie pointed Benny out to me, deep in furtive discussion with two angry men. One was young, the other old enough to know better. But he didn't.

Their discussion appeared to reach a natural conclusion and Benny, looking up, spotted Charlie and beckoned for him to come over. As I followed him, I noticed that the glares we had been getting from the egg men changed perceptibly as we were introduced to Benny's companions.

'Terry Fowler,' the elder one fairly growled in a deep cockney accent, offering his hand to us both. 'And this,' he said, patting the younger man on the shoulder, 'is my boy Scott.'

Charlie and I introduced ourselves nervously and were immediately besieged by a lengthy exaltation of the virtues of Britishness. 'But these fucking foreigners,' Terry Fowler explained, 'they just don't fucking get it and they don't fucking belong. They should just fuck off home.'

Benny, reading our reactions, was keen to play it down. 'This isn't a racist party,' he said. 'We just believe in "rights for whites". There is a crippling case in this country of what the establishment would call positive discrimination. That is what we object to.'

The Fowlers looked in awe at Benny's articulation of

their prejudices before Scott added, 'That, and fucking pakis.'

And he and his father guffawed, before walking off to the bar with their hands draped happily round each other. Benny, looking exposed, excused himself to go and talk to a friend who had just arrived.

I turned to Charlie. *'What the fuck?'* I muttered. He looked embarrassed.

'Mate, I swear I didn't know it would be like that, that's not how Benny made it sound, I thought it was just a party. Let's go,' he said.

And we would have done but then it happened. Then I saw love eclipse hate in the blink of an eye. There she was – floating straight towards us.

Do you believe in love at first sight? That two people can be drawn magnetically to one another and that free will goes out the window? That fate exists? That two can be one? Charlie didn't but her smile converts him.

It was the most beautiful smile he had ever seen – a smile that lit up the face of his love in its truest form. She had beautiful hazel eyes that held such light and sparkle that they made you forget where you were and who you are. Two moles adorned her left cheek and her chin – the joyous imperfection that gives true beauty a necessary semblance of humility. She had long, flowing brown hair that seemed to rise and fall like a beautiful symphony.

She was casually dressed. Well-worn trainers, light blue jeans and a white t-shirt with some dumb yellow slogan emblazoned across the front that Charlie, somewhat distracted, failed to read. I read it though.

'Hi, guys,' she said while I prayed that Charlie's jaw would arise from the floor. 'You're Benny's friends, right?'

'We're, um?' Charlie was struggling and I intervened.

'Charlie here,' I said, patting him deliberately quite hard on the back, 'is an old friend of Benny, and I live with Charlie. What's your name?' I asked.

'Rachel,' she answered. 'I'm Scott's girlfriend.'

Whether it was about hearing her name or the knowledge that she had a boyfriend, something penetrated Charlie like a cold shower and he came back to us and started acting normal once more. But I could still tell that he had fallen very, very hard.

Benny and Scott were working the room and so the three of us hung out together for most of the night. Rachel was incredibly good company and Charlie was on form like I'd never seen him before. I say that the three of us hung out together but really it was Charlie and Rachel and I was just an extremely interested observer. They had an instant connection; they shared a similar sense of humour and Charlie made Rachel laugh like she hadn't done in a long time. She sensed too, perhaps, that it was not the ridiculous politics that surrounded them which had brought Charlie there. He was a refuge from the rest of the party's reasons, a respite from the world that she had followed Scott into.

After a while Rachel produced a small digital camera. 'Take a photo of us,' she instructed me. I made sure that the dumb yellow slogan emblazoned across the front of her t-shirt could be seen and clicked. Rachel came over to see the result and seemed happy with it. It was a beautiful photo. The camera disappeared back into her handbag and we continued our revelry.

It was my round and so I made my way to the bar. There, whilst waiting to be served, I looked back at Rachel and Charlie and I could tell. You know how sometimes you can? You look at two people and sometimes they don't even know themselves. But you do.

I returned with drinks and the conversation lulled. I felt that it was because of my presence. I was intruding on something that belonged to those two. I still am. After a few minutes uncomfortably sipping our beers, Rachel asked Charlie to hold hers and disappeared in search of Scott.

I turned to Charlie. His eyes were alive and he shook his head at me in disbelief.

'*Mate!*' he said. Just that. Nothing more. And I understood.

'You quite like her then?' I teased.

'*Mate!*'

'And you're aware that she's both out of your league and she has a boyfriend?' I reminded him cruelly.

'Where there's a will there's a way,' he said trying to sound enigmatic. 'I just want to hang out with her some more. She's a cool, cool girl.'

'Yeah, she is,' I agreed. 'But when are you ever going to get to see her?'

'I'll get involved with this thing,' he said.

'The League?' I whispered contemptuously. 'These are a bunch of racist thugs,' I hissed.

'Yeah, but I don't believe that bollocks, I have an ulterior motive.'

We fell silent as Benny, Scott and Rachel came over to us. Terry Fowler, it emerged, had already left. It was Benny who spoke first. 'Sorry I couldn't hang out with you more tonight, boys; I had some organising to do. We're picking up the pace of our campaign.'

'No worries, mate,' Charlie said. 'It was good to see you again.'

'Did you have a good night?' Benny asked.

'Yeah, it was good thanks.' Charlie said. 'Listen Benny, is there anything I can do to help with the campaign? I'm keen to get involved if I can do anything to help.'

Benny looked at him suspiciously. 'Didn't think this would be your kind of thing, mate?' he said.

Charlie shrugged.

'Well, we've got some leaflets that we need to hand out. Scott and I are busy tomorrow but it would be good to start on that. Although it would be best if one of us were with you.'

'I can do it.' Rachel said suddenly. Everybody looked at her and she blushed, embarrassed. 'I mean, if you two are busy tomorrow, then I can bring the leaflets and Charlie and I can hand them out together. I'm free tomorrow, aside from an essay, but I can do that later.'

Scott and Benny looked at each other and the latter deferred to the former.

'Okay,' Scott said. 'That would be really helpful. But you don't have to, sweetheart.'

'It's fine,' she replied. 'You want all the help you can get, right?'

Scott shrugged and nodded.

'Well, that's settled then,' said Charlie, obviously ecstatic. Benny fixed him with a look of piercing suspicion but shrugged liked Scott.

'Well, we've all got a busy day tomorrow,' he said. 'Let's head home.'

We all said our goodbyes and Benny, Rachel and Scott headed up the road, while Charlie and I headed down, turned right past the mosque and entered our house. I talked to Charlie on the way back – I told him that this wasn't going to end well but he ignored me.

'Rubbish,' he said. 'This is the start of something

special.' We wished each other good night and hit the hay. I went to bed and lay awake, turning the night's events over in my mind. And I kept thinking of Rachel's t-shirt and it was then, I guess, that I realised that I had been given a story to tell.

Charlie went to bed well content. In his mind he had a date tomorrow with Rachel. Ideally, it would have involved more candlelight and dinner and less literature of hate but still, definitely a date. He closed his eyes with a happy smile on his face and he couldn't wait to meet the morning.

CHAPTER THREE

They met at ten o'clock outside a coffee shop in town. She was again dressed casually and again she was perfect. While still at a distance, Charlie took advantage of her looking the other way and stopped and watched her. She was wearing the same jeans and trainers as the night before but the white t-shirt with the dumb yellow slogan emblazoned across the front had presumably been changed, or was at least covered by a thin, black cagoule that kept out the drizzle. A backpack completed the outfit.

Charlie chuckled to himself that this assembly was so beautiful, that she was so beautiful, and that his heart was fluttering as he looked at her. She swung round her gaze and saw him where he stood and she smiled. He hurriedly broke into a walk and when he reached her, he brushed a kiss across her cheek.

'What were you laughing about?'

'Huh?' he said still lost in the aroma of her cheek. 'Oh, nothing.'

She looked at him with amused suspicion.

'I thought we could grab a coffee before we started,' she said.

'Sounds GREAT,' Charlie almost shouted, sounding distinctly like Tony the Tiger, and again she looked at him with curious amusement.

They ordered their absurdly named coffees and found two comfy chairs in the corner. Charlie stared resolutely into his mochalattecappuccinespresso™, occasionally glancing up to look at her when he thought she might not be looking. She always was. When the silence had become uncomfortable, Rachel reached in to her bag and handed Charlie a leaflet, distaste etched across her beautiful features.

Charlie looked at it and grimaced:

* * *

THE DEFENCE OF THE REALM LEAGUE

FACT! Extremist Muslims want to kill you
and your children.

FACT! Extremist Muslims form part of an international
conspiracy to undermine GREAT Britain.

FACT! Extremist Muslims want to rule our country and
make our women wear burkhas.

The Defence of the Realm League is a non-racist organisation, concerned with preventing the spread of radical Islamism in modern Britain, which threatens our way of life and seeks to impose upon us Sharia Law.

Our members come from many different backgrounds; White, Black, Gay, Straight, Male, Female and we are all united in our objective of defeating these extremists and restoring pride to our great nation.

We are tired of apologists making excuses for people who come to our country, use the liberties our ancestors have fought and died for and refuse not only to adapt to our way of life but actively seek to destroy it.

We have no problems with peaceful and moderate Muslims who wish to become truly British, and this is not a crusade against any race or religion.

It is simply resistance to an extreme ideology that threatens our values and our way of life.

"The world is a dangerous place to live in; not because of the people who are evil but because of the people who don't do anything about it."
- Albert Einstein.

JOIN US NOW AND SAVE OUR GREAT NATION!

* * *

When he looked up from the leaflet and into those beautiful hazel eyes, the paradox of his emotions jarred him physically. He looked at them and down at the leaflet again and felt sick with failed reconciliation. He wondered which would win.

'This is, um, quite colourful stuff, innit?' he said.

Rachel nodded in pensive agreement.

'Do you mind me asking,' he said, 'if you agree with all of this?'

'Do you?'

'I,' he exhaled painfully. 'I asked you first.'

'Okay, then. No. But I can stomach some of it. I strongly disagree with extremist Islam's subjugation of women, for example, and obviously I don't like extremists trying to attack us and well, look, that's about it to be honest.' It was a half-hearted justification.

'So you're involved out of duty to Scott?'

'In a way', she seemed uncomfortable with this admission of his influence. 'You?'

'I have no idea. Maybe duty to Benny.' Or desire for Rachel.

'You can leave if you want to,' she said.

He looked down at the leaflets and up at the eyes once more. The eyes won. It was no contest. 'No,' he said. 'Let's get to work.'

'This is not a racist organisation,' he told himself as he drained his coffee and stood up. He stepped into the drizzle. 'This is just about fighting extremism. It is a good cause.' He really did try to believe it.

They stood on a busy crossroads in the pedestrianised shopping section of town. It was a painful experience. He didn't know what was worse – the people who berated him for believing in something he didn't believe in, or the people who congratulated him for standing up for Great Britain.

In town, where they were handing out leaflets, there was a huge queue outside Upnorth Bank as people panicked to withdraw their savings. Charlie had a lot of success here – in fact, it was where he got rid of most of his leaflets that day. Perhaps they were bored and fancied a bit of reading material or were angry or worried and could relate to the cause. Who knows, but many of them took the leaflets.

Towards the back of the queue, somebody waved to him energetically. 'Oh, fuck,' he said to himself. It was Faisal, the man from our local newsagent who we were friendly with.

'What have you got there, Charlie?' he said in his thick Upnorth accent. 'Some good old anti-capitalist literature against these fucking banks?'

'Um, yeah, something like that, Faiz.'

'Give us a look then.'

'Err, I've run out,' said Charlie.

'Fuck off, I can see a big wodge stickin' out your pocket,' he said and playfully made to grab them. He got one. He read it. The muscles in his face seized up, his eyes hardened behind his glasses.

'What the fuck is this?'

Charlie gulped. 'It's not against Muslims in general, Faiz,' he explained shamefully, 'just extremists. It's…' but he stopped speaking as spit flew in to his face. Faisal ripped up the leaflet and threw the pieces at Charlie – a few stuck to the saliva.

'Don't ever come to my fucking shop again.'

Charlie was shell-shocked. He slowly wiped the spit away with his hand and wiped his hand on the back of his jeans. Rachel, who had been talking to an enthusiastick about twenty yards away, looked over at him and seeing his vacant expression, broke off her conversation and walked over to him. 'You okay?' she asked.

'Yeah, I think so.' Charlie looked at her, almost accusingly. 'I just got spat at.'

They repaired to a nearby pub and settled with a couple of pints in the corner. Charlie loved that she drank beer.

'Well, we got rid of most of the leaflets,' she said.

'Yeah.' Charlie was still dazed and hurt. He and Faisal had always got on really well and he had actively enjoyed going to his shop because he could always be assured of a friendly few words between them.

'Did you know the guy who spat at you?' Rachel asked perceptively.

Charlie didn't want to talk about it and so he changed the subject. He asked her about herself, Scott and Benny and the tangle of their lives.

CHAPTER FOUR

Life had been treating Scott Fowler well. He was approaching his last few months of school, he had a fun group of friends and his parents had announced to him, somewhat surprisingly, that he was to be joined by a baby sibling in the fall. And best of all, he was in love. It was the spring of 2005 and his relationship with Rachel had just begun – dawning with the leaves.

He really couldn't believe his luck. They had met at a street party in East London, close to his home. Although she was from North London, news of the party had gone viral online and so she had ventured across with a friend named Chloe.

A whole horde of teenagers had taken over the street and two cars had been parked across the road at either end of the party zone. Young kids drank alcopops and sucked self-consciously on cigarettes. The older teenage boys stood around acting lairy and chatting to each other on their recent discovery of dumb-bells and the inflationary and intimidatory effects that could be achieved by their use. The girls mainly stuck together but there was sometimes a lone girl, surrounded by a group of boys and relishing the attention.

Rachel and Chloe had barely been there twenty minutes when, inevitably, the police arrived to a chorus of boos and whistles. Rachel smiled at the muscular youth near her, who was chanting 'We shall not be moved', and he smiled back. They got chatting. Rachel asked him what would happen.

'We'll linger around for a bit, they'll make one or two arrests for breach of the peace or drunk and disorderly and then we'll be dispersed. Twenty minutes top.'

'Where else is good around here?'

'There'll probably be a bunch of people heading to Eastend Park if you fancy it.'

'What happens there?'

'We sit, we drink, we chat and then we probably get moved on by the police again.'

Rachel turned to her friend Chloe. 'Shall we go?' she asked.

It was still early and the party had been shut down so quickly that they decided that they might as well. Rachel informed Scott.

'Cool, well there's no point waiting around here,' Scott said. 'We might as well head now.'

And so they started walking. They talked as they walked and it took about ten minutes for them to realise that they hadn't introduced themselves, which they promptly did. At the off licence where they went to stock up, Scott bumped in to a friend of his from school who had also been at the street party but had left to get more booze.

'Pigs have come,' Scott told him. 'No point going back, come with us to the park.' So he did and, helpfully, he became interested in Chloe.

Rachel and Scott sat together on the bench in the park, exchanging the bottle of vodka. Scott was telling an amusing story in his endearing cockney twang and Rachel was laughing. *Really* laughing. A laughter so deep and so genuine and so consuming that it was convulsing her body and it was giving her a stitch. As she struggled for breath she leaned her head on Scott's shoulder for support and when eventually her breathing became a gentle pant, he raised up her head and kissed her for a long, long time. And to her it felt so natural, so beautiful, so right that the thought flickered through her mind that perhaps this was the start of her love story.

At the end of the night he and his mate, Gary, walked her and Chloe to catch the last tube home. They swapped numbers and Scott kissed Rachel good night. He watched her disappear down the steps to the underground and stood there for a minute after he could see her no more. He walked home, grinning stupidly, and lay awake for a few hours thinking about her before sleep overcame him.

From the very next morning they were texting feverishly about anything and everything. But mostly it was about their determination to meet up on Friday. In the end they agreed that Scott would pick her up from school and then they would spend the evening together.

She couldn't concentrate in class throughout the week, but Friday was the worst. The whole day was a dream that her teachers kept trying to wake her from. None succeeded. She was popular with the teachers and so she wasn't punished but a couple of them, peering out of the staffroom window, saw her skipping across the playground after lessons, and throwing her arms around Scott who was waiting at the gate.

That evening, they went again to Eastend Park where they had gone to the previous weekend. There was a funfair and they headed towards it. They crashed into each other on the dodgems, ate that disgusting monstrosity they call candy floss, and kissed on the big dipper. Scott tried to win her a teddy bear at the hoopla stall but had not managed after numerous attempts. He seemed quietly devastated but made it up to her shortly when he won one at the hammer game, and she chose a large stuffed replica of Thumper from Bambi. She clutched it happily for the rest of the evening, eating her McDonalds one handed, and cuddled it in bed that night.

They became best friends. Their love blossomed with the spring. Every night they would meet up after school. Sometimes he would go to North London, sometimes she would come East but in both places, if the weather permitted, they would spend their evenings in the park.

In East, they would return to the bench by the pond where they had gone on the night they met and here they would often be joined by friends of Scott and they would, like many teenagers, hang out. This involved doing, literally, nothing but listening to inane banter.

When they met in North London, they would most often be alone. They found a spot on a hill in the park beneath a huge oak tree where they would lie down together and talk until sunset, when they would sit up in silence to watch the end of another happy day. They both loved how long it took for the sun to creep towards the horizon before seeming to accelerate as it touched before disappearing completely in seconds. When it departed, they would feel a pang of sorrow but they would kiss in the afterglow and await again tomorrow.

As summer approached, sacrifices were made. Scott had his A levels and Rachel her AS levels and on the pragmatic insistence of the latter, they met much later in the evenings. But they still met and because the days were longer now, they still had time to watch the sunset. In fact, it was the best possible end to a day of revision, and its promise would sustain them through those sessions.

They gave themselves something else to look forward to as well. They booked a holiday to a Balearic island for the week after they finished their exams – just the two of them. And what a week it was! It was the happiest that Rachel had ever been. Waking up next to Scott every day was the perfect start to her mornings. They normally made love before getting up and then they would have breakfast together before strolling hand in hand down to the beach where they would spend their mornings frolicking in the ocean and reading to each other on the beach. After a light lunch their schedule would vary.

For their last afternoon, they hired a moped and went up in to the stunning hills of the island. Rachel's hair flying, her heart soaring, her hands around the waist of Scott, her cheek nestled against his back as she watched the scenery rush by. They ended up in a rustic *cantina* in a random village and by a mixture of sign language, pigeon Spanish and the flurrying of euros, they were soon enjoying wine and tapas. They fed each other bits of chorizo and olives and cheese and gulped down the wine.

As evening came, a couple of men began to play music – a guitar and an accordion filled the air and Rachel and Scott danced, to the delight of the locals who then proceeded to show them how it was really done. A woman in her late middle age took a shine to Scott and dragged him up for a dance. Rachel smiled and laughed as she watched him tread on the poor lady's toes.

They returned home very early on the morning of July 7th. By eight in the morning they had reached Scott's house and had just missed his parents leaving for work, his Dad going to the building site, his mum to her secretarial job in the city. Knackered, they went to bed to get a couple of hours' kip. When Scott awoke, Rachel was still sleeping peacefully beside him and he rose from the bed and went to the kitchen. He made coffee and toast for both he and Rachel and went back up to his bedroom, placing the plate and mugs on the bedside table beside her head. He got back in to bed and, spooning her from behind, he awoke her with insistent kisses.

She kissed him back and smiled, saying, 'Good morning gorgeous,' before stretching as she turned towards him and opening her eyes. 'I was just dreaming about that moped ride we took in the hills,' she said. 'I can't believe that was yesterday.'

'Good dream?'

'Of course,' she said and kissed him again.

'I brought you some coffee and toast,' he said.

But Rachel wasn't in the mood for coffee and toast. She clambered astride him. When they finished, the coffee was cold, the toast was soggy and Rachel offered to go and make some more while Scott took a shower. As she was waiting for the toast to pop up, she flicked on the telly and was confronted by the devastating reports of that terrible morning. She slowly absorbed the information running along the bottom of the screen and the toast popped up. She ignored it. The kettle boiled.

Scott entered the kitchen, his hair wet, and approached her where she stood loquaciously speechless.

'What's going on?' he said but she didn't answer him and he too absorbed the information from the bottom of the screen and the pictures in front of him. That bus. That picture of the blown-up bus. That lurid devastation.

He reacted first and pulled his phone out of his pocket. He tried calling his Mum but couldn't get through. He tried his Dad but again no answer, all the lines were jammed. Rachel was trying her friends and family but no one could get through to anybody and this, more than anything, instilled fear. They had become so accustomed to constant communication that they felt alone with the TV, relying on that antique to keep them informed.

Scott eventually had the presence of mind to try his Mum's office expecting her, as the secretary, to pick up the phone. She didn't.

'No, she hasn't arrived yet, Scott. I wouldn't worry though,' the voice said uncertainly at the end of the line, 'everyone's late, they can't get here.' Everyone's late or everyone's dead. He finally got through to his Dad.

'Have you been in touch with Mum?' he said.

'No, I can't get through, son. All the lines are jammed.'

Scott said nothing and his father tried to reassure him. 'I'm sure your mother's fine; it's just a communication problem.'

'Ok.'

'Listen, I'm coming home, son, ok?'

'Ok.'

'See you in a bit, son.'

Scott hung up.

Rachel had managed to confirm that her family were all safe but they had still not been able to reach Scott's Mum. Terry Fowler was home now and they all sat around the kitchen table, watching the TV, phones in their hands. Grim silence floated through the air until every once in a while one of them would confidently predict that Mrs Fowler was about to walk through the door. And then there would be a noise of somebody walking past their house and all eyes would be raised expectantly towards the front door but the jangle of keys never came.

As the morning became afternoon, Rachel rustled up lunch for the Fowler men, but after a few bites each they just prodded their jacket potatoes around the plate with weary pushes of their fork.

The helpline was useless. There was simply no information. Rachel tried the hospitals directly but this too was futile. There was nothing to do but sit and wait and as afternoon became early evening, everybody began thinking the same thing.

Call it a cliché but it is immeasurably true – it's the not knowing that gets you. Your imagination goes into frenzy as you think of a million scenarios with a million conclusions. You think one minute of a comedy of errors leading to the silence on the line – a flat battery or something, then the next minute you think perhaps she has run off with a lover and are happy because at least she is not dead. Then you think that she's gone, she was in the wrong place at the wrong time and was blown to smithereens.

You try to suppress this one and go for a realistically achievable compromise. She hasn't run off with a lover and she's not dead, but she was caught up in it. She's unconscious, perhaps, in hospital – but she's safe. Or she has some heinous injury and her life will never be the same again. She's lost the baby maybe but you guiltily don't care so long as she's ok. You make deals with an uncertain God. 'If she's okay, big man, you can have my soul and add it to the others. What do you do with them all anyway?'

But there's still silence. Silence, uncertainty and fear.

Thursday turns into Friday.

The first victims are named and her name does not appear. Joy and hope surge cruelly through you. More are named and still not her. You struggle for sympathy for the others but then feel resentful. At least they fucking know – it's the not knowing that gets you.

Nobody sleeps on Thursday night. Rachel manages to coax Scott to bed but he can't sleep. He lays his head on her chest through the night and she strokes his hair. She tries to console him and drifts in and out of sleep. As the sun dawns, they rejoin Terry in the kitchen. He hasn't moved and the TV is still on but his head is drooped towards his chest. As Rachel puts on the kettle, he awakes with a frightened jerk and breathes sharply. He looks around and sees Rachel and Scott looking at him and he tries to recover his composure.

The vigil continues. Rachel makes breakfast and the wait goes on. Rachel makes lunch and there's still no news. Outside, the weather is sunny and children are playing in the street. Inside, the curtains are drawn and that grim silence still chokes the three prisoners of fear. Rachel leaves the kitchen to make some phone calls but when she returns to where the Fowlers have barely breathed, she is still unable to offer them comfort or closure. The wait goes on.

Darkness descends on Friday and Rachel orders pizza. Again, the men eat little. Terry moves for the first time in hours and returns clutching a full bottle of whisky. He places three glasses on the table and pours them all a large measure. Rachel tries to decline but Terry orders her to drink. He makes a morbid toast and drains his glass.

The straight whisky, Rachel's first, courses through her like poison – not dulling the senses but momentarily amplifying their receptivity to pain and loss. Terry pours three new measures. Rachel sees no point in declining and drains her glass.

The moon is in the sky outside but is shrouded by the clouds. Rachel tries to coax Scott to bed once more but he refuses. He wants to stay with his Dad and Rachel feels like an intruder on their grief. She retires to bed alone and in the morning she wakes, feeling guilty that she has enjoyed a good night's sleep.

Friday is now Saturday. She descends to the kitchen and finds Scott asleep with his head on the table. Terry is awake and holds a glass of whisky in his hand. He has not slept. He looks up at Rachel and begins to speak. He announces that he was always the last man standing at a wake and Rachel can think of no reply. She judges his resistance and prises the glass from his hand. She drags him off the chair and is almost crushed under his weight as she supports him through to the sitting-room and lays him down on the sofa. When she returns with pillows and a blanket he has passed out, but his unconscious face is full of lines of pain.

She returns to Scott in the kitchen and gently nudges him awake. He asks what news and she shakes her head in reply. More victims have been named but Mrs Fowler's name does not appear. Suddenly, Scott turns optimistic. He just knows that she's alive, he says. She wouldn't leave us. I know she wouldn't. Rachel tries to soothe him but he is fiercely insistent. I know it, he declares. I just know it. But as morning becomes afternoon and he stews in silence his optimism evaporates.

Rachel cooks a fry up which Terry re-emerges to eat. A new bottle of whisky is on the table and Rachel tries to gently dissuade him from drinking it but he knows better. And he forces the others to partake as well. Saturday night descends and for the first time they all go to bed. Terry takes a bottle with him and clutches it in place of his absent wife in their bed that's made for two.

Saturday becomes Sunday and Rachel leaves Scott asleep in bed to go downstairs. She makes herself coffee and cleans up the kitchen. The TV yields no news. There is no sign of Terry. She feels aged by the last three days and stifled by the house. She opens the front door and sits on the step, lighting a badly needed cigarette. A man in a suit is walking up the road and she watches him. He is looking at the house numbers and consulting a piece of paper in his hand. He opens the gate in front of her and stares at her hazel eyes.

He asks her if this is the Fowler residence. She says that it is. His face contorts with genuine compassion and Rachel knows what news he brings. She cries for Scott's mother and for Scott and for Terry and she hears footsteps coming down the stairs. It is Scott and he looks at her inquiringly and she shakes her head at him with tears streaming down her face. He looks at the man in the suit and the man says he's sorry. Scott's hands fly up to his face and he violently collapses to the floor, writhing in agony. Rachel rushes over to him and he sobs against her breast. The man in the suit closes the door between them and sits down on the step, overcome as a witness to their sorrow. Terry Fowler emerges from his room.

Terry Fowler skipped grief for the most part and reacted with rage. He and the geezers down the pub would discuss how 'them fucking pakis' needed to be driven out of the country back to where they belonged. And many of the geezers in the pub agreed with him either on principle or out of sympathy to his loss. Very soon, they were encouraging him to get involved with fringe politics. 'No point trying to get the main parties to listen, Tel, they're a bunch of fucking pussies. Them Nationalists though, they got the right idea.'

And so Terry did join them, and found that many members were sympathetic to his anger, and many more actively shared it. Scott wasn't interested in getting involved. He was too consumed with grief to leave the house, but he agreed with much of what his father was saying and passively approved of his decision to enter politics.

Rachel went over every day after work but she couldn't seem to get through to him. She listened to his increasingly angry rants about 'them fucking pakis' and chided him softly for it. Their sex life ceased. He wasn't interested. He never thought about ending it with Rachel because he never thought about her at all in that time. His thought process could not move beyond his sadness and a vague and lazy hatred of 'them fucking pakis'.

And she never thought about ending it with him because she appreciated the huge grief he was experiencing but believed that it would end. She remembered how happy they had been just a short month previously. In short, she was still in love with him. She stuck with him and showed the enormous strength and weakness of her character.

She tried to speed up the grieving process by encouraging him to go out but he refused. It was almost September by the time she managed to get him out of the house for a night on the town. He insisted he didn't want to go, that he wasn't ready, but she insisted more.

'Please,' she pleaded. 'Do it for me.'

She needed this. It had been a tough time and she needed to get out and let her hair down. She needed to believe that normality could return, that they could go out and have fun like they used to. That Scott was still the same person she had fallen in love with.

Grudgingly, he relented. They started off in Scott's local pub in East, The Queen Victoria. Scott's friends were there and they were all trying to distract him from his grief. They tried to lift his spirits, to raise their voices, to prove that they were carefree spirits just out for a larf.

After a few drinks, they moved on to a bar on the high street, where the drinking continued, but still Scott didn't say much. He just sat and drank in glum silence.

Rachel asked him to dance.

He refused.

She asked if he minded her going for a dance.

He assented.

The others went with her and they all messed around, pulling deliberately goofy moves that matched their smiles. Scott watched them. He saw an Asian guy checking out Rachel and he took a long pull of his beer. He watched the guy approach Rachel and say something to her and he watched as Rachel smiled and shook her head. He took another pull of beer and began to peel off the label as the guy retreated. He downed the rest of his beer and went up to the bar, ignoring the stuff at the table he had been assigned to watch.

He had a shot at the bar and ordered another. As it arrived, he looked across to the dance floor and saw that the Asian guy had returned and was talking insistently again to Rachel.

He downed his shot and walked over to the guy. He crashed his fist into his face and the guy fell to the floor. He jumped on top of him and crashed his fist down again. And again. Again. Again. 'You fucking paki cunt,' he screamed. Rachel half succeeded in pulling him off but he pulled away from her and returned to his victim. He landed another few punches before the bouncers contained him. The guy's face was a mess. A mishmash of blood and lost teeth and glazed eyes – for he had slipped out of consciousness.

When the police came to take Scott away, Rachel was crying so much that she felt she might never stop. Before he was ushered into the police car, Scott turned to Rachel and said, 'It's your fucking fault. I told you I wasn't ready to go out.'

And she cried harder still as the police car drove away.

CHAPTER FIVE

Benny looked at his new cellmate suspiciously.

'Alright, mate,' said Scott.

Benny glared at him. 'I ain't your mate.'

'Fair enough,' said Scott. He sat down on his bunk in silence.

Benny managed to keep up the hard arse routine for about twenty-four hours but in the end he couldn't help taking Scott under his wing, like he had taken Charlie under his wing at Downsouth. On the second night they shared the cell and prompted by the boredom of a bad book, Benny finally spoke to Scott.

'What are you in for?'

'GBH.'

'First time?'

'Yep.'

And as soon as this was said, Benny couldn't resist befriending the new boy. It was in his nature. Like he had done with Charlie, he told Scott tips for survival and the best way to get through the days.

He also recounted the story of his own incarceration, and Scott laughed heartily at much of it. In fact, it was the first time he had laughed properly since his Mum died. Benny laughed with him, but his laughter was shallow and at the end of the story, when he told of Charlie's betrayal and his separation from Sally, his voice had become hard and bitter.

After a while, Scott confided in Benny. He told him the story of his mother's death.

'And I'm just so fucking angry,' Scott said. 'I never knew real anger 'til Mum died. Why her? What the fuck had she done to them? She was innocent. And my baby brother or sister? I swear to God, man, every time I think about it, I just want to kill the fucking lot of them.'

As we know, Benny was sometimes capable of great compassion, and now it was misguidedly directed towards Scott.

'Well, if you do that,' he said, 'you won't change anything and you're just gonna spend the rest of your life here. There's smarter ways to get your own back, without having to completely fuck up your own life.'

'Yeah?' Scott flared with anger. It was always close to the surface these days. 'Politics, I suppose?'

'Something like that.'

'It's a waste of fucking time. It's just a load of boring old men talking. I want action. My Dad's gone down that route and it's a load of bollocks. He goes round knocking on doors and holding meetings and wearing a suit. It's just so *acceptable*.'

'But what about a movement that's not just about talking? It's about action too. It's not just a rejection of Islam but a rejection of the political process as well.'

'How do you mean?'

'Kind of like a gang. We change the game. We don't wear suits and sit in boardrooms – we take to the streets. We let out our anger, we have a scrap.'

'With who?'

'Anyone who fucking fancies it. There are plenty of angry young men out there. We find them. We mobilise them. We banish extremists from our country so no one ever has to go through what you did again.'

And Benny made him believe. He had to make himself

135

believe first but, once that was accomplished, he could make Scott believe. Or a whole host of people. He had always had great powers of persuasion.

It was there in that cell that the League was born. Together, they thought of ways to promote their cause. They began networking with like-minded people who were in the joint with them. There were plenty of them. And they pursued it with vigour – it breezed them towards the end of their sentences. Benny, after three life changing years, was the first to be released.

Scott had given Benny his father's contact details but Benny was holding out. He gave himself one last chance of salvation. For all the anger that was surging through him, there was still one deep vein of tenderness. Of true purity. The first thing he did when he got out was to get a train to Downsouth. Sally Chadwick could still save him.

As the train rolled through the complacent greenery of the Home Counties, Benny looked out at it, smoking rollies. The spacious expanses of verdant pastures mocked his bitter years under lock and key and a deep resentment flowed through him. The ticket inspector asked for his ticket and his resentment increased. He snarled as he showed him.

The train rolled through familiar stations and he counted how many were left until Downsouth. He tried to think of what to say to Sally but had still not found the words as the train rolled in to Downsouth. He walked from the station to an exceedingly grubby pub he knew close by. He and Charlie had often come here, safe from snobbish teachers who would never venture there. The bar staff had changed in the three years since he was last there but there was one old man sitting at the same stool where he had been every time Benny had ever been there. The old man showed no sign of recognition and Benny wondered how much his physical appearance had changed. It was a considerable amount. This was the first time Benny had ever had a legal drink – he was of age now. Older, even.

Over his first pint of freedom, Benny held a pen hovering over a piece of paper and tried to write down what he wanted to say to Sally. After his first pint was finished, the paper contained just a few scribbled false starts.

Over his second, he managed three consecutive sentences. He read them back to himself and scrunched up the paper in to a tight ball. It was too late to start rehearsals, he decided. He'd winged it all his life and he'd wing it now. He ordered a third pint, drank it quickly and left the pub.

He began the climb up the steep hill towards Downsouth. He didn't even know if Sally still lived there. He made towards Chadwick's house and paused, panting, outside the front door.

He knocked and heard Chadwick's voice inside call, 'Will you get that, Sally?' She answered, 'Yeah, coming.' So she was still there. He heard her footsteps come quickly down the stairs, he saw her shadow behind the door and looked in to her eyes as she opened it. Her eyes held shock. There was a silence.

'Who is it?' called Chadwick from inside.

Sally's voice stuttered but she eventually managed to call back, 'It's for me, Dad.'

'Is it Horatio?' She ignored him and stepped outside closing the door behind her.

'Hi,' said Benny. 'Not going to invite me in then?'

There was hostility in his voice that he didn't mean to be there but out it came anyway.

'Dad,' she offered in explanation. There was another silence. 'So you're out then?'

'This very day,' he answered.

Her heart beat wildly as she realised that he had come to see her immediately.

'What was it like?' she asked.

Benny gulped. 'It was hard, Sally. It was really hard.' Bitterness and anger had again crept in to his voice and it scared her. 'The things I saw. The things they did to me. And I did it all alone. Why the fuck didn't you visit me? Or write? Or call?'

'Benny, I'm so sorry. I couldn't.' She was struggling to speak and her breathing was laboured. 'It would have been too hard. It was hard enough having to think about you every day. I had to try to forget you.'

'Did you?'

'No, Benny. I could never forget you.'

'Did you get with someone else?' The tone was angry and accusatory and held the premonition of the answer.

There was the danger of heartbreak written all over him and she couldn't go through that again. She couldn't. She was afraid. She'd made her bed.

'Yes,' she said finally.

Benny gave a slow nod. 'And if I asked you to come back to me to finish what we started?'

She shook her head ruefully, 'I can't, Benny.'

He grabbed her hands, suddenly tender, 'I need you,' he pleaded. He was crying. Tears filled her eyes but she continued to shake her head. 'I can't live without you,' he went on. She remained silent and Benny swelled with rage.

He grabbed her face and tried to make her look into

his eyes. She refused to meet them, and Benny knew that he was defeated. 'Well, I don't fucking need you anyway,' he spat into her face. 'You fell through on me like everybody else.'

He forced a kiss on to her lips and walked away. And that was it. It was the last time he ever saw her. She stood on her doorstep crying and shaking and Benny, being Benny, returned to the pub.

He must have stayed there for a long time but couldn't precisely remember what happened. What he did know was that it was morning and he had woken up in a bush beside a canal. Bleary, he called up Terry Fowler.

''Ello?'

'Hi, Mr Fowler, my name's Benny Stone. I'm a friend of Scott.'

'Yeah, Scott told me about you. He said you might call yesterday?'

'Yeah, sorry. There was something I had to do. Scott said you might be able to put me up for a while?'

'Of course, Benny. A friend of Scott is as good as family. You in London?'

'I will be in an hour or two.'

'You got the address?'

'Yes, Mr Fowler.'

'Terry, please.'

'Okay, well I'll be with you by about midday, Terry.'

'Fine, Benny, fine. Looking forward to meeting you, son.'

And he hung up.

He rang the door bell and Terry Fowler answered. He was a thickset man with a substantial beer belly that stuck out of a plain white t-shirt. His face was red and he had a closely shaved head of greying hair. His face lit up as he saw Benny and he gave a Mafioso gesture of welcome with his hands before patting him on the back and inviting him in.

'So how's my boy Scott?' he asked.

'Yeah, he's getting on fine and he'll be out soon.'

'I know, I know. I can't wait. I've missed that boy.'

They went inside and Terry offered tea. As Benny drank it, he listened to Terry's explanations of his political activism with the nationalists.

'Things are really picking up here in East, I reckon we've got a good chance of taking it at the next election. Nick's confident anyway. He's a great man, he is,' he said affectionately. 'Scott was mentioning that you guys are thinking of getting involved?'

'Well,' Benny replied. 'We're thinking more along the lines of a youth protest group, unaffiliated to any political party. But our ideas are the same. War on extremist Muslims.'

Terry was encouraged. 'I'm real glad Scott met you. I told him that he had to *do* something after what them paki cunts did to us, but he never seemed interested.'

And after that, Terry treated Benny like an adopted son. And Benny, who had never known his father, reciprocated. He followed Terry around, helping him with his activism and met some of his cronies. He thought of plans for the League, which began to solidify. He discussed them with Terry in the pub and received an enthusiastic response. He talked of action and Terry replied like a radicalising imam, 'I'd love to be doing that. Unfortunately I've got too many other things to do but, really, I'm very jealous.' Yeah, right.

They lived alone together for almost three months

before it was the day of Scott's release. Terry and Benny went to pick him up and they all drove back to the Queen Vic for drinks. Many friends of the Fowlers were there and, after a while, Rachel arrived. Scott saw her standing by the door and he walked over to her.

'Hey,' she said.

'Hey.'

'Welcome home.'

'Thanks.'

There was a silence before Scott spoke again. 'So how've you been?'

Rachel pursed her lips and nodded as if weighing up a deal. 'Yeah, okay I guess. I've applied for uni.'

'Where?'

'Upnorth.'

Scott didn't know exactly where that was but it sounded far away. He didn't press the issue further, but spent the evening gently reacquainting himself with Rachel and slowly rekindling her feelings for him. Eventually he apologised to her for what he had said the night he was arrested and she, in her forgiveness, went home with him that night.

Benny's friendship had fortified him and he was, at times alone with Rachel, almost the same old Scott. He began to re-imagine his love for her and resolved to cling to her forever. She was a happy remnant of better days. He decided to follow her to Upnorth and, as he sat in the Queen Vic with Benny one afternoon, he explained his position. Benny, though privately disappointed, put on his thinking cap.

'Well, why don't we go too?'

'To uni?'

'Yeah, we've both got alright A levels.'

'But we haven't applied,' Scott reminded him.

'Let's try and get in through clearing,' Benny suggested. 'Bit of further education and it's a damn good place to push the League. That's the heart of the matter up there; that's where some of the bombers were from. We'll take the fight to them.'

Scott liked this plan and they went about the paperwork. Benny got in doing sociology and Scott, not knowing what to choose, imitated him. Rachel was not exactly overwhelmed by the realisation of this idea but there was still love in her heart for Scott. She couldn't shake off the nostalgia of their previous happiness and hoped that away from London, and from Terry Fowler in particular, she might get her Scott back.

CHAPTER SIX

But the sands were shifting. And as the winds blew Rachel and Charlie closer together, they drifted away from Scott and Benny.

Rachel and Charlie would still meet up, ostensibly to do the leg work for the League, but piles of leaflets would end up where they belonged (in the rubbish) and the two would just spend the day together in a café or a pub, telling each other of their lives. And of their hopes and their dreams.

Scott and Benny were also spending all of their time together and, with the encouragement of each other, were ever radicalising their radically retarded logic. Their ambitions became more lofty, their delusions greater and with no one there to keep them in check, it became more and more certain that their folly could end only in tragedy.

The sanctity of friendship is a strange one – it seems to celebrate love, loyalty and affection and yet it is dangerous. Just as blind loyalty or eternal allegiance to one political party is dangerous, because they too are like shifting sands.

And as people we are forever shifting, changing, developing, regressing. Sometimes at pace with our peers. Sometimes not. But the sanctity of friendship, which is also the sanctity of love, appears to demand a blind allegiance that is greater than reason or logic. Nonsense logic anyway.

And then there is history too, that eternal struggle. Because of our inherent inability to reconcile history, it is the wrongs of the past and not the necessities of the present that often guide our reason. So, historically, Charlie did something terrible to Benny. He betrayed him and tore him from Sally. And he still feels guilty about this. But is Benny the same Benny that he left in that bus? Or is Charlie the same Charlie that left him there? Or is Scott the same person that Rachel fell in love with? We all stand on shifting sands, which means that the people we lean on for support, those who are closest to us, will inevitably change over time. To cling to them fully, perhaps we have to learn to realise when the others have gone. That we are grasping at thin air.

Rachel and Charlie had reached out in to the blankness and had grasped each other. In December of 2007, they went ice skating on the temporary rink erected in the centre of town. Rachel had asked Scott first but he declined with a snort. 'Ice skating's for fucking poofs.' Charlie went happily. He had never been before and was utterly hopeless but Rachel, laughing, took him by the hand and led him round and round.

Occasionally, she rushed off in a graceful burst of acceleration and rejoined him after an express lap to where he had shuffled along about ten feet, fearfully holding on to the rail.

She took his hand again and pulled him along on her own momentum. Charlie became excited, 'I'm doing it,' he squealed. 'Look at me go.' Rachel relinquished her grip and immediately Charlie overbalanced, then overcorrected and finally accepted that he was going down.

'Are you okay?' Rachel asked, half inclined to laugh.

'I think I've bruised my bum,' he said, rubbing it contemplatively. She got him to his feet and didn't let go of his hand until they were safely off the ice ten minutes later. Charlie, who had been utterly petrified throughout the experience, was enthusiastic as soon as it was over. 'We should definitely go again,' he said as they walked in search of dinner, her arm linked through his. 'I really felt like I was getting the hang of it.' Rachel stopped walking, looked at him and burst out laughing.

'What?' he protested.

As 2008 dawned they began to go to the cinema together, or bowling. They went to cocktail bars and out to dinner. They talked with voluble excitement about nothing and everything. They arrived at exhilarated conclusions to their conversations and an awkward silence would follow. They sipped at their wine. One would break the silence with affected mundanity and the other would embrace the delaying of that final truth.

On more than one occasion, they were out alone together and a stranger would voice an assumption of their relationship. A barman, on seeing Rachel take out her purse to pay for her round, joked to Charlie, 'Letting your girlfriend pay for the bevvies, eh? Good man!'

'Oh no, she's not…'

'He's not…'

They looked at each other, embarrassed, and then back at the barman whose smile was widening and they said at the same time, 'We're just friends.'

'Fair enough,' the barman grinned. 'Five forty, please, love.' And Rachel paid him and they scurried off to a table in the corner.

'Who could ever think we were an item?'

'I know! Ridiculous, innit?'

Yeah yeah. And they took safety slurps from their pints.

At that time, Upnorth was experiencing a musical boom

and two local bands in particular had been transformed into international stadium acts. The trickle down effect was that somewhere in the city there was always a gig going on, and it was usually good.

If they were at a loose end, they would go to one and together they discovered new bands. It was a unifying experience. We all need companions on our adventures, for what is the use of experiencing something wonderful if we have no one to share it with?

It became one of their bonds. They would play each other music on their mp3s, each one desperate for the other to share their love of a new-found band. And normally they did share it. And it would show as they danced together at the gigs in simple synchronicity, embracing the excuse for physical contact. They had been disciplined in maintaining platonic boundaries, despite Charlie's momentous yearning because he didn't have the courage of a kiss.

I'm not sure if their self-deception was total but it certainly seemed that way. Benny and I had known from the start of course, perceptive outsiders as we were, but there was another player who appeared blinkered to the facts. Scott, in his disinterested attitude towards Rachel, was complicit in her growing relationship with Charlie. He just didn't seem to think it strange that it was Charlie, and not him, who was actually dating his girlfriend. His focus and energy were poured almost entirely in to the League.

He had, however, recovered his sex drive and when his loins urged him on, he would dispassionately fuck Rachel. She would watch him get dressed as soon as he had finished and leave the room without a word or a single shred of tenderness. Tears trickled silently from haunted hazel eyes and meandered across her used and naked body.

It was a couple of days since Charlie had last seen Rachel and he was missing her like it had been decades. She hadn't returned his calls and Charlie was becoming worried that he had done something to upset her. He was in the union bar waiting for me when he saw her sitting on the terrace outside, reading the paper with a coffee and a cigarette. He went to speak to her.

'Hey,' he said. 'What are you up to?'

'Oh, hey,' she said, glancing up. 'Just killing time before my next class.'

He noticed something about her face.

'Rach,' he said.

'Yeah?'

'What happened to your face?'

Her left eye had been heavily made up but it still betrayed a telling bruise. Her hand shot up there instinctively.

'Oh, is it noticeable?' she asked. 'I was wearing socks on our kitchen floor and slipped and wacked my head against the sideboard. The swelling's gone down loads though.'

'Ouch,' Charlie grimaced. 'Are you okay?'

'Yeah, fine,' she said casually.

'Rach. Is that what really happened?'

She looked up at him quizzically. 'Yeah, why?'

'It's just that…well…it looks like somebody's hit you.'

'What are you trying to say, Charlie? I slipped and fell and hit my head, okay?'

'Okay. It's just…It wasn't Scott, was it?'

'What the fuck, Charlie? No, it wasn't Scott. Scott would never do that to me.'

He paused. 'Okay. But if it was, you'd tell me, right?'

'Wrong. It's none of your fucking business.' She snatched up her newspaper and her bag. 'I'm gonna be late for class,' she said and left without another word. She rushed past without noticing me as I was walking into the bar. I looked at Charlie. He shrugged.

CHAPTER SEVEN

By the time we started our final year of university in September 2008, the world was whirring around us once more. Now I don't know much about economics but it seems to me that a few days after Charlie's twentieth birthday, the economy was what is technically described as utterly fucked up.

There was a strange atmosphere in the air. It had been lingering since the run on Upnorth Bank the previous year but had been partly dissipated courtesy of government/ taxpayer intervention. Now it all came rushing back and people started swinging.

I watched with envy when, across the pond, people started to swing in the direction of Hope and Change – the two buzzwords of this time. I can't deny it; I was utterly enamoured by the rhetoric too. It's a shame that it was only rhetoric.

Over here, things were a bit bleaker. People were swinging as well but to extremities. Very many swung left, especially amongst the students of Upnorth University – there was a surprising resurgence of Marxism. But many also, propelled by the forces of anger, swung towards Benny and Scott. You could see the two sides shaping up.

Throughout that autumn, the tensions increased. There was an outbreak of violent assaults on Asian men in the city. One of the culprits was caught and identified as a member of the League but Benny defended the League eloquently enough:

'That this man was a member of our organisation is

purely coincidental. We are a non-violent protest movement, and this man's actions were his own individual concern.' And presumably it was a concern of his victim too, but never mind that. The other problem with this explanation was that it was a flagrant lie.

Charlie was dimly aware of an increasingly extreme ideology within the League but he thought it was very much a fringe movement. Little did he know that Benny and Scott were actively seeking more and more violent recruits, men who loved a scrap over anything. Their greatest success was when the Upnorth Uglies – the city's feared football firm – joined *en masse*. And they knew some people in turn.

The gatherings were incredible events that made the first one, which I had gone to with Charlie, look like a tea party. Lager soaked chants of white supremacy filled the air and it is fair to say that they didn't resemble the meetings of most 'non-violent protest movements'.

The Christmas holidays applied a welcome brake to the tensions, as various protagonists drifted home. And it was too cold for big public gatherings anyway. December is a funny thing in England – it quietens the nation. Or more precisely, it diverts their attention from national battles to the sometimes stormier domestic front of the family.

When we returned to Upnorth in January, we had the most important exams of our lives so far to sit. Scott and Benny, who had all but abandoned their pretence of attending university, didn't bother, but the rest of us were revising like crazy and it temporarily blocked out the wider issues of the time. Charlie, Rachel and I were together a lot at this time as we had some of the same exams and all favoured working in a particular part of the library. They were hectic but happy times and rather than distracting each other, we spurred each other on and rewarded ourselves with a drink in the evening. I often felt like a third wheel at these drinks but they always insisted I accompany them.

Coming out of our final exam in January, Charlie, Rachel and I went to the union bar. For once the TV was not showing bitches and hos shaking their booty and tang to da badass get rich quick tunes of contemporary American hip-hop. There was a different black American on the screen and we watched together his inauguration as the 44th President of the United States.

I don't know what it was; the incessant hope of it all probably, but Rachel and Charlie kept exchanging what I interpreted as hopeful glances. I remembered the dumb yellow slogan emblazoned across the front of her t-shirt the night they met and smiled happily because, in my eyes, Rachel and Charlie finding happiness in each other was just around the corner and I so wanted their happiness. I really did.

But for some reason it didn't happen then. Charlie still hadn't plucked up the courage to let her know that he was madly, overwhelmingly, emphatically in love with her and it was always going to have to be on his initiative that she broke free from her sense of duty to Scott. Maybe it was because I was there. Perhaps I was cramping his style.

The bar was alive with chatter once the inauguration was over. The students there were the ones who had finished their exams and what with that and the hope across the pond, the place was buoyant with jubilation. We had many, many drinks that night and it was, in a sense, one of the best nights of my life but it missed that crowning glory. It missed the realisation of love.

CHAPTER EIGHT

That weekend, Rachel's friend Chloe came up to visit her. Benny, Scott and Charlie were in the pub already and a couple of pints down when Rachel and Chloe arrived, dressed up to the nines. They had been a couple of hours getting ready and catching up, and they had the full and immediate attention of the boys.

Charlie felt the customary exhilaration when he kissed Rachel's cheek and then noted with interest, upon kissing Chloe's, that she had borrowed Rachel's perfume. When Rachel edged past him to sit between him and Scott and Chloe sat down on his left, he was surrounded by a sea of scent he loved.

The five of them, as often happens, commenced an all-inclusive conversation of the mundane before splitting in to their own conversations. Charlie had seen Benny take a passing interest in Chloe but there had only ever been one girl for him and Charlie had put an end to that. As Benny remembered Sally, he sought refuge in a conversation with Scott about plans for the League that took place in hushed tones.

Charlie, in an aromatic and tipsy daze, proceeded to talk to Chloe in a conversation like he had never had before. Suddenly, out of nowhere, he was charming, witty, eloquent and engaging and Chloe was hanging on his every word with delighted eyes and musical laughter at appropriate moments.

Rachel, separating these two groups, quietly observed both duets – the increasingly stormy baritones on her right and the hopeful tenors on her left. She said nothing until the time came for Charlie's round – the third – when she offered to accompany him to the bar, leaving Chloe alone and ignored by Scott and Benny. They stood by the bar and waited and Charlie turned to Rachel.

'Chloe's great,' he gushed. 'We're getting on like a house on fire.'

'Yeah, she is.' Her voice was cold and hard.

'What's up with you? You've been really quiet all night.'

'I'm *fine*. I just don't want to get in the way of you two lovebirds.' Her lips curled everywhere.

Oh my God, thought Charlie. Can this really be? Is this jealousy? If it is, I am *definitely* pushing for more – maybe she does care for me after all. But she seemed to read his thoughts and was quick to correct them.

'Listen, Charlie, I care about Chloe and I don't want her to get hurt. She's had a really rough time of it with guys lately. Be gentle.'

'What makes you think I wouldn't be?' he said, feigning offence. He caught the attention of the barmaid and ordered, faintly flirting as he did so, feeling in this moment like a true Don Juan. He turned back to Rachel and decided to push his luck.

'You're not jealous, are you?'

Her eyes flashed. 'Don't flatter yourself, Dixon. I'm worried about my friend, she gets attached easily. She is *not* a target for a one night stand.'

I'm gonna do it, thought Charlie. You can stop me if you want to. You know how. But if not, I am definitely banging your friend.

'Look,' he said, 'we're both adults and we can do what we like.'

Her eyes flashed again but she said nothing, grabbed two drinks and stormed back to the table.

It is safer to play chicken with cars than with love.

They were back at Rachel's house and Chloe was sitting on the sofa as Charlie poured them both a glass of red wine and sat down next to her. Rachel had gone back to Scott's house, not without a final look of warning to Charlie that he had ignored triumphantly. They were alone. It was just him and Chloe and he turned to face her on the sofa.

'Cheers,' he said, raising his glass as she mirrored him. They had both drunk a lot that evening but Charlie's sense of control had, for once, not deserted him and he knew exactly what he was trying to do.

'Chloe?' he said. 'If I tell you something, do you promise you won't laugh at me?'

'Of course I won't'.

'It's just,' and he counted an appropriate fake pause in his head. 'I wanted to tell you.' Now for a qualifying excuse. 'I mean, I've had a lot to drink but…' Last little pause before a charmingly understated compliment. 'I think that you're lovely.' Fake bashful smile, look down, look up, note smile, lean a tiny bit in and BRAKE…not yet. That was close. Phase two. Top up wine. Give her a chance to speak.

'I've had a really good time tonight,' she said. 'And I think that you're lovely too.' She seemed on the point of saying something but let it stew for a while. Was she fake pausing too? 'I haven't been very good at finding lovely boys historically,' she said.

Don't let her explore this avenue too thoroughly, that way danger lies.

'Well, we're not all bad,' Charlie said glibly, knowing full well that in this moment he *was* one of the bad guys.

'My intentions are honourable,' he assured her jokingly.

'Kiss me, Charlie.'

No way does that ever happen in real life but fuck it, there he leans and smoooooooch.

'That felt nice,' she said as they parted. Charlie said nothing but stood up with his wine glass, offered her his other hand and led them up to Rachel's bedroom where Chloe was to be sleeping. Rachel's bedroom! Oh, the joy and the justice of it all! He anticipated the scent on the pillows and prayed furtively for an overlooked pair of panties on the floor.

You, Charlie Dixon, have fallen into bad ways.

But of course he went and did it. He went and fucked her. Twelve minutes of dull, loveless sex and another person hurt. Five minutes of post-coital snuggling later and Chloe went and said it. The three words he'd been waiting for his whole life. He mumbled something in reply, rose from the bed, ran out the front door and sprinted home bollock naked in the rain.

Charlie's waking thought was 'Why I am always either drunk or hungover?' Next was, 'What the fuck happened last night?' And then memory visited him and so did Rachel.

He heard the knock and went to answer the door, still in his birthday suit. Rachel looked at him and then looked down, pulled a disdainful smirk-grimace, slapped him hard across the face and told him to put some clothes on. This he did, and when he returned downstairs he found Rachel disgustedly inspecting the grime of our kitchen.

'I was gonna ask for a cup of tea,' she said, 'but there don't seem to be any clean cups.'

'Rach,' he started, 'I'm sorry about last night…'

She cut him off. 'It's not me you've got to apologise to, dickhead.'

'Look I'm sorry, I got scared, I bottled it, she said the L-word,' he finished feebly.

'Fucking hell, Charlie, are you ever gonna grow a pair? Or behave like an adult? Or think about other people's feelings? Or *care*? I told you she'd had a rough time and to go gently but you acted like every other dumb male prick I've ever known.'

'Is she alright?' he asked more from fear than compassion.

'Well, I hope so – she called me after you left her and I went round there and spent the night trying to console her.' Bags under Rachel's eyes attested to this. 'She really liked you and now she thinks she's unlovable. I think I managed to convince her in the end that you are a dumb, shallow, scared, mean little bastard who's definitely not worth it and I hope she realised that it's true.

The words stung and stabbed him coming from the mouth he most treasured but he knew they were true and he knew he deserved it.

'I'll go round now and apologise,' he said.

Rachel nodded silently and then she took his hands and said, 'What is it with you, Charlie? You're two different people. What do you need to vanquish the wanker?'

He needs you, Rachel. Tell her. Tell her, you fucking idiot, you coward. Tell her.

And although he knows it, he doesn't take that leap of faith. Why is he ashamed of love? It is only the madness that haunts us all, the illogicality that makes us human. So why not? Is he too scared or too naive? It doesn't really matter which, he's got all the time in the world to pluck up the courage.

156

Charlie was dreading going round to see Chloe but he knew he'd been a shit and he knew it had to be done. He knocked on Rachel's front door and Chloe answered.

'Oh, it's you,' her voice mingled with contempt and surprise.

'I came to apologise,' Charlie declared nobly. 'Can I come in?'

'I guess.'

For someone who Rachel had said was a wreck a few hours previously, Chloe seemed remarkably chilled out as she closed the door behind Charlie and followed him through to the kitchen. She even offered him a cup of tea.

Charlie, who didn't want to prolong the interview but felt he should do exactly the opposite of whatever he wanted as a kind of petty sacrifice, awkwardly accepted. There was silence as she made the brews and Charlie spent the time looking at the photos on the fridge – or more precisely, he spent the time looking at the photos that contained Rachel on the fridge. Chloe followed his stare as she laid the cup of tea down in front of him and, seeing that he was distracted, had to remind him why he was there.

'You came to apologise?' she said.

'Hmmm?' Charlie then emerged from his daydream. 'Oh, yeah. Listen, I'm really sorry,' he limped.

'What for?'

So it was gonna be like this, eh? Okay then, fair enough.

'For the way I behaved last night.' Charlie slid smoothly into pomposity. 'It was despicable of me, and I feel like an utter prat. No one deserves to be treated like that and I am deeply, truly, sorry.'

'It's okay.'

'Really?'

'Well, it was my fault too. I thought you were different, you see. I should have realised you were just like all the rest – just another fronter.'

A fronter? He had not heard the term before but it struck him as acutely appropriate. 'Well, yes, I guess I am,' he said. 'But that doesn't make it any better – in fact, it makes it considerably worse.'

Chloe shrugged her shoulders and Charlie tried to take a sip of tea but it was still piping hot and he realised uncomfortably that this again would prolong the interview. 'The fact is,' he announced, 'that I should never have led you on because…well, because I'm in love with somebody.'

'So why aren't you with *her* then?' Chloe asked coolly.

'Ah, there lies the problem. She's with someone else, so I don't imagine she feels the same way,' Charlie said self-pityingly.

'Have you told her?' Chloe asked.

'Have I told her what?' said Charlie, his eyes drifting back to the fridge.

'Have you told Rachel that you love her?'

Hot tea swept through his mouth and came gushing out of his nose and Charlie's eyes watered. Chloe grinned and raised her eyebrows. She got a piece of paper towel and held it to Charlie's nose. She put on a baby voice, 'Blow for me, Charlie, *there's a good boy.*' Charlie blew. There was only one person in control of this conversation. She mopped up the tea-snot on the table as Charlie tried to recover his composure. She returned to the table and sat down. Charlie avoided her gaze.

'Well?' she said. 'Have you told her?'

'Of course I haven't. She is amazing and beautiful and wonderful and I'm me.' There was an excruciating amount of self-pity in his voice.

'I agree that seems to be a huge discrepancy but for some strange reason, I think she quite likes you.'

'And what about Scott? He'd kill me.'

'Scott has made his choice. He's chosen this ridiculous debacle with that clown Benny. I know you and Rach are mixed up in it too but I know you don't really believe that bollocks. Neither do they really. Scott's just angry and Benny just loves the contrarian anarchy of it all. And you two are just there out of some nonsensical feelings of guilt and duty and a desire to spend time with each other. The whole lot of you are quite pathetic really.'

Charlie nodded silently. 'You picked all that up already?' he finally said, impressed.

It was Chloe's turn to nod. She met Charlie's eyes. 'Tell her. Scott and Benny are gonna go to the bitter end with this but you can pull Rachel out before it gets seriously out of hand.'

'Maybe she doesn't want to be pulled out.'

'You won't know until you offer.'

Charlie nodded silently again and looked up at Chloe. 'You're quite amazing, Chloe.'

'I'm not falling for it twice, Charlie.'

'I'm not fronting. I'm just saying that some day, you're gonna make a very lucky guy, very very happy.'

'I don't need your sympathy, Charlie.'

'You're right. You don't.' And he smiled at her, drained his tea and walked out the front door.

When he got home, Rachel was no longer there and, in fact, he didn't see her for some time. She was avoiding him as if she knew the end was coming.

CHAPTER NINE

Meanwhile, the shenanigans of the League were developing at quite a pace. The rhetoric was becoming more inflammatory and the Upnorth union had decreed that they were no longer allowed to gather on campus. Benny and Scott were incensed but they found support from an unexpected corner. They found it from me.

I wrote a preaching article for the Upnorth News. You know the type surely – I lazily misquoted Voltaire and invoked the spirit of democracy and freedom of speech. Blah, blah, blah. And unexpectedly, it worked. A referendum was held on campus and the decision was reversed. The League was once again free to try and preach their hate. They failed, of course, because they were attended by so many protesters who drowned them out with chants that nobody could hear a word. So they were banished from campus the right way.

It was not, in a way, dissimilar to how Terry Fowler's boss, some months later, was controversially allowed on to a prominent television programme and was so utterly dismantled by a very bonnie lass that his whole show began to disintegrate.

Students might be a tiresome bunch but you can usually trust them to be a vague moral compass for a nation. And incidentally, they shouldn't have to pay nine grand to perform this duty.

Benny and Scott, determined as ever, took to the streets of Upnorth once more. They held a succession of small rallies in the centre of town, which always stopped just short of violence. It was close though. A loose band of unaffiliated anti-League protestors always attended and the police were all that separated the two factions. Benny was turning into quite the orator and at these events he would speak with Scott and some other lieutenants standing by his side:

'People of Upnorth,' he would shout. 'How long will you stand idly by as foreign forces corrupt our country? As they try to kill our fathers and mothers, our sons and daughters? There is a battle raging beneath your nose and it is time for you to pick a side. What legacy are we to leave to our descendants? Will they grow up in a country under the evil influence of Sharia law or will you join us? Will you accept your duty to defend our values as your forefathers did?

'Three score and ten years ago, we were threatened with an evil foe and our ancestors stood tall and proud and faced down this evil with courage and integrity. Our time has now come and the enemy is more dangerous. For the enemy is within. He slyly lives among us and tries to sabotage our way of life. He lives on benefits from the taxes we pay to support him while he pursues his full-time job of undermining us. His mission is our destruction and our mission is our salvation.

'How will history judge you? Did you stand on the sidelines and let our nation be destroyed? Did you passively watch our values denigrated? Were you the reason our women wear veils of shame? And were you responsible for the demise of the bacon sarnie?

'Albert Einstein once said that, "The world is a dangerous place to live in; not because of the people who are evil but because of the people who don't do anything about it." I ask you today – what kind of person are you? Are you the type to fight for freedom? I believe in the people of our great nation and I believe that they will accept their responsibility. Join us. Save us. Reclaim our fair Albion from the hands of wicked men. Thank you.'

A raucous sound of mingled boos and cheers would erupt from those gathered and Benny would glibly accept the congratulations of Scott and the others. There would be other speakers and after a few hours the League would march, chanting, through the streets of Upnorth to a pub where they would do what they do best – get pissed on lager.

Charlie tried to get more involved with the League again. He was hoping to see more of Rachel but still she stayed away. In fact, she spent much of that time with me. We bumped into each other in the library and began to go for coffee breaks together. I never said much, I just listened. Damn, I'm a good listener. This entire narrative is composed from what Charlie and Rachel told me.

I suppose it was my duty to link them together but somehow I never really got round to it. I could vaguely see how the plot was developing and it seemed interesting enough to write about. Plus, I'm not one to interfere. Anyway, she told me of her life and I carefully recorded what I heard.

One day, after a long and boring session in the library, I went up to her and asked her if she fancied unwinding over a drink. It had been a long and boring day for her as well and she didn't need much encouragement. She packed up her stuff and we walked to the union bar.

After several pints, I was feeling pretty tipsy but Rachel seemed the same as ever and she immediately spotted Benny and Scott, when they walked in to the bar. I half expected them to be holding hands, so close were they these days but, then again, that wouldn't have been very macho.

They came over to us and Scott greeted Rachel with a kiss. Benny turned to me and thanked me for the article I had written to get them reinstated on campus.

'I didn't do it for you,' I told him. 'I did it for freedom of speech. Nothing more. Your League is a bunch of racist thugs but I just wanted the public to have a chance to realise that.'

Scott answered for Benny, 'What did you fucking say?'

The beer answered for me, 'You heard me. I think you're both fucking idiots. I think your League stinks of shit and I think that Rachel here deserves someone a hell of a lot better than you.'

I was spoiling for an argument, not a fist fight, but the next thing I knew, I was on the deck and blood was pouring from my nose. I assume it was Scott who punched me but I really can't say for certain. As I looked up, dazed, they were both hurriedly walking out the door and Rachel's beautiful face was over mine encased in concern. I felt better at once.

In April, Benny announced a massive rally in Upnorth to take place on the May Day bank holiday. Members of the League from all over the country, people from similar minded organisations and unaffiliated sympathisers were expected to turn up in bulk. It was to be the biggest event in the League's history and it was Benny's baby – the culmination of his anarchic delusions.

The forces were being assembled on both sides. I was working with *Unite*, an anti-League group who were gathering pace and supporters in their attempt to face down the League. The build-up was tense, and so were my relations with Charlie. I repeatedly tried to convince him to abandon his folly but he had hardened against me. He had found out that I had been seeing a lot of Rachel without telling him and he felt betrayed. But if I hadn't let him into my confidence, then I wasn't the only one.

When he had got over his initial anger at my liaisons with Rachel, I tried to glean information from him about the League's plans but he didn't know anything. Benny, wisely, didn't trust him and it was he and Scott who were formulating the tactics for the League. And if the rumours were true, their plans were becoming more dangerous as they egged each other on and spoon fed each other delusions.

Scott was in scant contact with Rachel – she watched fretfully from the sidelines as he and Benny grew secretly bolder. Bolstered by their many new recruits and these recruits' violent ideas, they managed to convince themselves that they were at the forefront of something big. They imagined thousands of like-minded souls throughout the country, ready, waiting for somebody to make a move. They dreamed of revolution.

CHAPTER TEN

The day before the rally, Charlie plucked up the courage. I don't know what inspired him to do so but he did. I think he realised that he was being frozen out by Scott and Benny and that the League was no longer a route to Rachel. He resolved to go over to her house.

He found her in a state of great agitation. She seemed to be on the edge of a breakdown – perhaps she was. Years of anxiety bubbled inside of her as if she could sense – perhaps she could – the coming climax of the fall of the angry young men.

'Where are the boys?' Charlie asked.

'They went out,' she replied, looking at him with what looked a lot like fear. 'They haven't told me anything but they're planning something bad for tomorrow. What is it?' she demanded.

'I have no idea.'

She paced the room furiously pushing buttons on her phone. She looked at Charlie and she was shaking and there was fear in her eyes. 'Their phones are off. Something bad is gonna happen. I know it, I can feel it.'

Charlie offered his comfort and she accepted his embrace and as she breathed heavily in to his shoulder, he stroked her hair and whispered reassuring words into her ear.

'Let's get outta here,' he said. 'I'll drive.'

She nodded fitfully, grabbed her cagoule and gave the keys of her battered old Mini to Charlie.

They drove in silence – once or twice she seemed to

make small movements of her hand towards Charlie's on the gear stick but her eyes were fixed on the outside world and the drizzle that deposited raindrops on the window. They drove out of the city, leaving behind the broken industry and the urban chaos and past green fields and sweeping hills. The England of poets.

The Mini feebly ascended the gradients and Charlie eventually brought it to a halt on the edge of Upnorth Moor. Rachel seemed to awake from a trance and turned to Charlie and asked a silent question.

Charlie opened his door, got out and opened hers. He offered her his hand and said, 'C'mon, I've got something to show you.' She took it uncertainly and they left the car and walked uphill on foot. His breathing became heavier but hers appeared to ease as she took in the beauty of their lonely solitude.

Not a soul was in sight. The hill flattened and Charlie led her through a thin cluster of pine trees and down a gully. He appeared to know his route well although he had never visited this place before.

They came upon a stone ledge by a stream that was quenched by a waterfall gushing merrily beside them. He turned to face her and stared into her hazel eyes. Their pupils conversed in the silent language of love and no words needed to be spoken. Away from the chaos of their lives both finally understood, relented and conceded to the bare fabric of nature.

They faced each other, holding hands above the covers and both looked deep in to the other. They saw each other's happiness, they saw the realisation of a dream and they saw love.

'I always knew.'

'Me too,' Rachel purred softly.

'From the very first moment I saw you. I couldn't drag my eyes away from yours.'

'I've replayed that night in my mind so many times.'

'Me too.'

'You remember that picture we took that night?'

'Yep. I tried so hard to look at ease.'

Rachel laughed beautifully, 'You failed. You looked petrified.'

'I was. My whole life I was a sceptic of love and my whole world just flipped. Have you still got the photo?'

Rachel smiled bashfully. 'I got a hard copy made the very next day and I've carried it around in my purse ever since. Do you remember what I was wearing?'

Charlie searched his memory, inundated with her image. He remembered what had been of so little importance in the face of love: 'Trainers…light blue jeans…and…a white t-shirt…with some dumb yellow slogan emblazoned across the front. To be honest I barely remember where we were. Why?'

'I bought that t-shirt earlier that day and haven't worn it since, but that dumb yellow slogan emblazoned across the front actually acquired some significance.'

'What did it say?'

'You should remember,' she teased kindly.

'I had just fallen in love with you! Fickle fashion didn't seem very important then!'

'I promise to wear it on our first date.'

'Deal.' Charlie leant in and kissed her and she wrapped her arms around him and pulled him close.

When he awoke, she was no longer there. For a minute he was struck by the terrible thought that it had only been a dream. Then Rachel rushed through the door fully dressed.

'Have you seen this?' She looked at him with fearful eyes and handed him his own phone. He read the text message on the screen. WHERE THE FUCK HAV U BN? 2DAY'S THE DAY. WE'RE GOING ARMED. B THERE. BENNY.

'What the fuck?' Charlie said. 'What are they playing at? This has got to be a joke.'

'It's not.' Rachel said. 'I got a voicemail from Scott and he was all tense and excited and told me to stay away. We've got to stop them.'

Charlie thought for a moment. 'No,' he said. 'We've made our choice. We stay.'

Rachel looked at him astounded. 'Benny's your friend,' she shouted. 'We have to stop them. Somebody's gonna get killed. I'm going,' she said and before he could stop her she was out of the door.

'Rach, don't,' he cried futilely. 'Fuck's sake,' he muttered as he jumped out of bed, threw on some clothes and chased after her.

As he ran down the road, he saw her get on a bus that had just pulled up outside the mosque and he was sprinting to get on it but it pulled away. He reached into his pocket for his phone to call her but realised that he had left it in the house. As he despaired, another bus pulled up and he hurriedly got on. The ten minutes that it took for the bus to get into the city centre were the longest of his life.

It was easy to spot Scott and Benny. They were where the chaos was. A line of riot police several officers deep was blocking the way, repelling the angry crowd. Scott was at the front, shouting at the crowd, screaming at the police, his face contorted with rage. Benny was next to him, pushing futilely against the shields of the police. Charlie recognised other faces in the crowd – a savage army of angry young men that he had helped to assemble. They surged against the uniformed wall and those who fell fended for themselves. The sunlight reflected off sharp metal in their hands and Charlie felt a premonition of death, although he did not know for whom the bells might toll.

He could see Rachel in front of him, pushing valiantly through the massed ranks of thugs. A petrol bomb flew over her head and exploded near Scott, wounding a police officer. She quickened her pace and Charlie struggled to keep up. As a second petrol bomb landed within police lines, the men in uniform started using their batons with vicious rigour, their faces now mirroring the angry hordes. One policeman with fire in his eyes foolishly broke ranks and the mob quickly encircled him, leaving him trapped and isolated and looking into the psychotic eyes of Scott as he fearfully drew a knife.

The police were desperately pushing forward to get their man back but were met with fierce resistance led by Benny. Six of the thugs had now relieved the lone officer of his shield and his baton and he stood helpless in front of Scott's nervous knife.

By now the police were closing in on one side and Rachel from the other. Charlie was still struggling to keep up but he kept pushing through and could see now that almost forty angry young men were waiting with drawn knives for the main bulk of the police to arrive.

And still Scott did nothing. His eyes were no longer filled with rage but with fear as the skirmish burst into life. The police had broken through at last and the battle raged. The forty knives flashed wildly through the air, few hit their mark and Scott and the lone officer had seconds until the battle engulfed them. Benny was screaming, 'Do it now!' and Scott's arm was raised and the hand was steady and the life of the officer flashed before his eyes but the blow never came.

Charlie watched helplessly as Rachel reached Scott in his moment of fury and swung him around and away from the police officer as he brought the knife down and he plunged it through the heart that Charlie held dearest. The police swooped on Scott who had dropped his knife in horror and offered no resistance as they took him away. He looked back to see Rachel cradled in Charlie's arms.

'Rachel, Rachel!' Charlie wailed. 'I'm so sorry, it's all my fault.'

The lights in her eyes flickered as she gasped her final words. 'I'm sorry,' she whispered. And she exhaled. And the lights went out.

CHAPTER ELEVEN

This was Charlie's second funeral and it felt like his own. He stood at a distance as the tearful throngs entered the church. It was a better turnout than his grandmother's. Of course it was – we claim to value the young. He watched the coffin go in and felt an impulse to wrench it from those black-clothed shoulders and prise it open for a last embrace. He slipped into the church and stood at the back.

It was packed in the church and Charlie was not alone at the back for there weren't seats for everyone. He recognised some faces and hoped they would not see him. And he was convinced that he saw the same woman dressed in red who had stood out at his grandmother's funeral amidst the black. And once more her face contorted and mascara dripped from her eyes, brushed her cheek and fell to the cold, stone floor of the church.

Occupying the front rows were Rachel's family and he ached with guilt as he gazed upon their sorrow. And he panged once more as Rachel's eleven-year-old sister began to read the same verse that he had read for his grandmother. Her father came up to help her finish it as she struggled but she waved him away in the graceful manner of Rachel and tearfully ploughed through until the end.

Two waterfalls of tears plunged from the depths of Charlie's eyes. Or deeper. And a man at the back who worked for the undertakers stared at him. And stared. And stared. And Charlie left.

He went to the graveyard where he marched past Rachel's empty pit to the far corner where he sat down on a grave. He noted that this man had died young and wondered if the hearts that loved him still wail as his did now. Yes, Charlie, they do.

Still, he was not as young as Rachel whoever he was and as Charlie tearfully choked and spluttered through the cigarette he had lit, they brought her into the graveyard and the words floated almost inaudibly to his unseen, morbid retreat.

The coffin was lowered and the earth was shovelled upon her and the priest read out some formulae. When it was over the crowd dawdled, then dwindled, then departed.

And Charlie approached. He knew no one was listening but he had to say something, to speak to her. If only God existed.

'I miss you,' he started, 'more than you can know. I'm glad I told you just in time how I loved you from the very start. From the beginning. Always. And forever. But I'm sorry for the time I wasted. I'm sorry that I didn't shelter you from that very first moment. That I allowed the circus to continue. That I allowed you to die. I'm sorry.'

The effort of admission was too much for him and he crumpled over the earth and his tears soaked it and he inhaled some of the wet dirt through his running nose until a hand stroked his hair and lifted him upwards.

The teary hazel eyes he looked in to matched his grief but they still somehow cared for this world, and for him. It was Rachel's mother. She pulled him into an embrace and he sobbed pathetically into her shoulder.

She whispered as she supported him, 'She loved you too. Please don't blame yourself. Look at me.' She pulled his face towards hers. '*I* don't blame you. You were the only thing that made her happy whilst she was trying to help poor Scott. She never talked of him, only of you.'

'I failed her,' Charlie groaned.

'You did no such thing. You loved her and that was all you could do. Look,' she said as she pressed a folded bit of card in to his hand. 'This was the only photo in her purse when she died. Keep it, and treasure it, but please don't blame yourself.'

And she relinquished her hand and her bodily support and Charlie almost fell as she walked away. He opened the folded photo – it was from the night they met – and he ignored his love infused grin. And hers. And her t-shirt with the dumb yellow slogan emblazoned across the front and was drawn as always to her eyes.

Oh, those beautiful hazel eyes!

He couldn't bear to see them. Few have the power in their eyes for their sparkle to be caught on film. But hers did. And his wept. And he tore them away from hers and folded the photo and placed it in his suit pocket.

Oh, those beautiful hazel eyes!

CHAPTER TWELVE

'Numb me,' thought Charlie. 'Placate me. Sedate the sorrow of my soul. Give me peace. Give me death. Give me drugs. Lots of drugs.'

He was back in Upnorth again, his finals were over. Some exams he managed to attend, others he just didn't bother. But he had still received, in the post, notification of his attainment of a lower second-class degree. God, it's easy to get one these days, they just dish them out to anyone. Even to a mournful, developing drug-addict.

Charlie moved permanently to our sofa. I wanted to keep an eye on him but I didn't do a great job. I had got myself a decent degree and like the rest of my generation was finding it really useful – while I stacked supermarket shelves. And I was busy scribbling away in my spare time, thinking how fortunate I was to have my subject living with me. So maybe I didn't try that hard. As I said before, I watched the fall of Charlie Dixon with distant sympathy. Call it artistic detachment – or falling through on a friend. So I watched him.

He lay on our sofa drinking his vodka, smoking his weed, popping his valium and snorting his ketamine. Not coke. No way. That was for white collar wankers and bankers who somehow ignored the blood on their hands as they racked up their endless lines of life support. I bet he's on it now though. Ketamine was different – a truly nihilistic experience of nothingness. Charlie would deliberately take too much, k-holing his way through hours at a time.

And when he came round he would drink some vodka,

smoke a spliff, pop a valium and watch daytime television. Occasionally, while watching some dire Australian soap opera, he would burst into tears and weep and weep inconsolably until his eyes were dry and stinging and then he would drink some vodka, smoke a joint, pop a valium and snort a line of horse tranquilliser.

And the court date loomed sometime in the uncertain future. Fuck, the process was slow. And he wanted it to be over and for Scott Fowler to be put away for the rest of his hateful life. He wished they still had capital punishment, he wanted that fucker dead. So he had lied. He recalled his original statement:

'Scott knew about Rachel and I,' he had said. 'He was angry and bitter and jealous. And I saw him as Rachel ran towards him, I saw how his eyes lit up with glee as she approached and he was ready with his knife, so that when she reached him, it was with a smile on his face that he plunged that blade into her heart.'

The defence, on the other hand, had told the truth. Scott was in way over his head. He had been filled with anger and hate by the death of his mother years previously and had joined his father's reaction of rage. He was guilty of killing her and he would plead guilty but Rachel was never the intended victim and it certainly wasn't premeditated. He had been facing the stranded police officer and had still not attacked. The defence claimed that he only raised his knife, not to kill the police officer, but to *do* something as the leader of the mob surrounding him. And he was running out of time, the police were closing in and he was scared as a pair of hands pulled him round and he recognised Rachel when it was already too late, when the fatal blow had already been struck. Shocked, he surrendered silently to the arriving police officers. He was

175

truly sorry, he had loved Rachel and would never have hurt her even if he knew – which he didn't – that she had spent the previous night with Charlie.

Charlie knew that his false version of events was adding to his guilt but he was filled with such hate that he just didn't care. It would go away, he thought, with another drink of vodka, another valium, another doobie and another line of ket.

This went on for months. For Charlie, the days seemed to simultaneously drag by whilst managing to merge seamlessly into one another as in an endless nightmare. And it was a nightmare – a terrible dream state of numbed awareness that still, in all its horror, was preferable to the sharp edges of a reality without Rachel. I did try, I swear I did, but maybe not that hard.

'Let's go to the pub, mate,' I would say. 'Get out of the house for a little bit.'

'Maybe tomorrow,' he'd reply and I thought, okay then, at least now I've got time to do some more scribbling for this damn book. So I left him to wash down a valium with vodka and chase it with a joint or some ket or whatever the fuck he wanted to do with his life it wasn't my responsibility I had my own life to lead I couldn't look out for my friend all the time and it was his own fault and not mine it's not I promise it's not I tried my best I did I did.

Breathe.

'Charlie?' I peered in to his dull eyes but they made no movement or sign of recognition. My heartbeat quickened.

'Charlie?' I said again and I picked up his wrist and I felt for a pulse. I felt nothing and I dropped his arm and it fell limp off the side of the sofa.

'Charlie?' I asked once more but in no more than a whisper and I closed my eyes.

A clammy palm grasped my face and as I opened my eyes, Charlie's face had contorted into a ghastly grin and he said, 'Oh! It's you!' and laughed.

'Fucking hell, Charlie, you scared the shit out of me, what the fuck are you doing to yourself?'

His grin began to fade as he registered the tone of my voice.

'Don't live like this, Charlie,' I pleaded with him. I wanted a happy ending for my book, I really did. He wasn't a tragic hero but a clown and this was a farce so surely, surely the genre would assert itself and things would fall into their rightful place.

Tears welled in his eyes as he realised, perhaps, that he was hurting me too. 'I can't do it,' he said wiping his right eye with his sleeve. 'I just can't, I'm sorry.'

'You can, Charlie, I'll help you. You've still got plenty to live for. Come on, mate, *try*. We'll get out of England, see the world, go volunteer in Africa, have adventures, live life to the full…'

This wasn't the ideal time for a knock on the door but I left Charlie to his thoughts on the sofa and answered it. There was something familiar about the man's face I looked into. It seemed to hold the final, tired defeat that Charlie was edging towards – it was a face that once held naive, romantic ideals which had long since been tamed in a tedious triumph of pragmatism. Still, his suit suggested that pragmatism had its perks. I noted all this in silence as I stood before him, barring entrance.

He raised his eyebrows expectantly. 'I'm Charlie's father,' he said. 'Can I come in?'

'Erm well…'I stuttered as my arm fell from the door-frame and I let him pass. I followed James Dixon through to the lounge where he stopped suddenly and watched his son light a spliff. Charlie's eyes looked up and met his father's. Time stopped.

I saw Charlie through his father's senses. His hair was long, greasy and matted. His face was adorned with scraggly stubble. He smelled distinctly of sweat and other excrement. His skin was the palest white, except for under his eyes where blue bags were the bruised remnants of months without night or day. Before him on the table was a litter of empty bottles of pills and vodka, strewn tobacco, filters, empty baggies, cans of lager, an overflowing ashtray that was originally a dog bowl. There was a haunting, raspy quality to his breathing. His phone, which had run out of battery several weeks ago and had yet to be recharged, held scores of unanswered parental messages of concern and others from Scott's prosecutors. Everything suggested that he had scuttled himself.

Time restarted. James Dixon was flying towards his son and in a second he was over him. He lifted him by his t-shirt and aimed a punch at Charlie's face. In the very last fraction of a second his fist began to change direction and so only brushed Charlie's cheek. It couldn't have been that Charlie moved; he was too paralysed by drugs and fear. The spliff had fallen to the floor.

James Dixon regained his composure, let out a deep breath and sunk into the sofa beside Charlie. He didn't smoke normally but he took one of Charlie's cigarettes that were on the table and lit it. He looked at me and then at Charlie and with a great effort he said, 'I'm sorry. I shouldn't have done that.'

We said nothing. He looked at Charlie with pity, disgust, shame, compassion and love. Those were the elements I could discern anyway.

'What's going on?' he said finally.

Charlie burst into tears. 'Nothing, Dad, I'm fine.'

'You don't look fine.'

Charlie buried his face in his hands. 'I can't do it any more Dad, it's too hard.'

James Dixon embraced his son. He looked up at me. 'How long's this been going on?'

I looked shamefully at the floor. 'A couple of months,' I muttered.

'And you didn't think to call?'

'I was hoping it would pass,' I said. James Dixon looked at me with disbelief and shook his head that somebody could fall through on a friend so spectacularly.

'And do you live like this too?' he asked me.

'No, sir.'

He shook his head again and stood up, hauling Charlie to his feet. 'Clean up this mess,' he ordered me. 'I need to clean up my son.'

I did as I was told and had the place looking spick and span by the time James and Charlie came back downstairs. Charlie was unrecognisable. The bags under his eyes remained and the eyes themselves betrayed dubious vitality but he was clean. And he was shaven. And he was wearing clean clothes – mine admittedly, but I didn't feel like raising the issue.

James Dixon pressed some banknotes into my hand and told me to go out and get some food – healthy food. Again I did as I was told.

When I returned armed with fruit and veg and some nice cuts of meat, Charlie and his father were sitting on

179

the sofa, with a pile of envelopes in front of them and Charlie's phone on charge on the table.

'What's all that?' I asked. Charlie looked up and answered me.

'Mail that got sent home. Mostly about the trial. I'm supposed to be in court the day after tomorrow.' His voice was fairly steady but his eyes were petrified.

James Dixon stood up and took the bags of shopping from me and inspected them. 'Let me rustle something up,' he said and I silently relinquished the bags and sat down next to Charlie as James walked in to the kitchen.

'The day after tomorrow?' I exclaimed quietly.

'Yeah.'

'That's pretty hectic.'

'Yeah.'

'You okay?'

'I think so,' but he seemed extremely uncertain as to whether he was or not. 'I have to meet the prosecutor tomorrow to go through what I'm gonna say.'

'You gonna tell the truth?'

Charlie looked at me intently. 'You took the same classes as me. You know that truth is subjective. The truth is that Scott deserves the worst.'

'Lying won't help, Charlie. And trying to punish him won't bring Rachel back.'

He flinched but tried to look vindictive as he replied, 'It will make me feel better though.'

No, it won't. Of course it won't. But our conversation had ended.

James had cooked up a very tasty looking stir-fry and after Charlie and I had laid the table, we sat down to the most civilised meal that house had ever seen.

'This is very good, Mr Dixon,' I said. I was sucking up but it was true. He ignored my compliment and turned once more to his son.

'So, Charlie, what now?'

'What do you mean?'

'What are your plans for after the trial?'

'I dunno.'

I butted in, 'Charlie and I have always talked about doing some charity work in Africa together.'

James looked at me briefly and then turned back to his son.

'Why don't you come home?'

'Okay.'

'I can get you a job at the bank.'

'Okay.'

Eurgh. Yuck. Nepotism.

'I think you'll enjoy it. The pay will be good and soon you'll be able to get your own place.'

'Okay.'

I was trying to catch Charlie's eye but he was concentrating only upon his food. Silence consumed the rest of the meal, and the once tasty stir-fry felt stodgy in my mouth. After we had all finished, James Dixon left for his hotel and I immediately confronted Charlie.

'Don't take it.'

'What? You're the one that's been telling me the whole time to sort my life out.'

'Not like this. You need to sort your life out – not give up on it.'

'Mate, are you *serious*? What choice have I got? I can't carry on living like this, that's what you've been telling me.'

'What about our dreams? About how we talked that

we were gonna do some good, however little – for some people, however few? What about Africa?'

'I can't do those things now, I'm a broken man.'

'So you're giving up on life. You twat.'

'I'm not, I just don't have the courage to live or die any other way.'

'No. What you are saying is that you are actively choosing a pale imitation of the joy and the sorrow of life because you don't have the bollocks to keep trying.'

'So what are you gonna do then, bigshot?'

'I'm gonna do some good, however little – for some people, however few.'

'Oh yeah, because you're such a nice guy… and how you gonna do that?'

'I dunno, maybe I'll actually follow through on our plans and go and do charity work in Africa. But I'm never giving up.'

'You'll capitulate too. We all do in the end.'

'Fuck that, dickhead. Just promise me to remember that life will open its arms for you. As soon as you dare to dream again.'

'Alright mate, whatever, enough with the Obama rhetoric, I'm gonna start packing my stuff.'

CHAPTER THIRTEEN

Early the next morning, James came round and picked up Charlie and his stuff. He got him a room in the hotel in the centre of town and they spent large chunks of the day with the prosecutor. I had gone to work when Charlie left and so we never even said goodbye. But I was determined to see how things turned out and so I called in sick the next day and went to the trial. I got there early because I knew it would be packed – the media were extremely interested in the case.

I was squeezed into the gallery for the start of proceedings and I looked down at the room, taking in the scene. Scott, in the dock, looked soberly anxious. The judge looked ridiculous – does fancy dress really evoke authority?

There were a string of witnesses questioned and cross-examined. Policemen and other people at the protest all gave similar accounts. Scott was about to stab the police officer but hadn't meant to stab Rachel. So he was up against attempted murder of the police officer, but it looked like Rachel's death would be counted as manslaughter unless Charlie managed to convince them of premeditation.

Finally he was called. He took the oath and stood fidgeting in the witness box. Not once did he look up at Scott.

The prosecutor was a youngish man in a suave, blue suit. 'Will you please tell the court your name.'

'Charles Dixon.'

'And what is your relationship to the accused?'

'We worked together in the Defence of the Realm League.'

Charlie appeared to have learnt his script well but I thought he was not putting much effort into his performance.

'And to his victim, Rachel Robinson?'

Now Charlie started to deteriorate. He was visibly moved by the name and the court waited patiently for his answer.

'She was, um,' he started painfully. 'She was, um.' Third time lucky. 'She was my everything. She was my best friend and the night before she died, she became my lover,' he burst forth, suddenly voluble.

'And did Scott Fowler know about your relationship with Rachel Robinson?'

'Yes, he was very jealous. Early on, when we first became really close, I have reason to believe that he hit her.'

There was a noise of protestation from Scott. He was silenced and the prosecutor continued.

'Why do you have reason to believe that?'

'She had a black eye.'

'And she told you that Scott did it?'

'Not in so many words.'

'Yes or no.'

'No. But I'm convinced he did.'

'Returning to the matter in hand. Why do you think Scott knew about your affair?'

'It was obvious. Both Rachel and I had disappeared. We could only be together. When Rachel swung Scott around at the rally, I could tell he knew. There was a manic glint in his eye.'

'So, in your opinion, this was a premeditated murder?'

Charlie's eyes flew up to me in the gallery and I mouthed the words 'Tell the truth.' I doubt he would have listened to me but it was enough to provoke a certain agitation. Charlie began to fidget uncomfortably and his hand flew into the pocket of his suit. He felt something there and a look of curiosity came across his face. He pulled it out. It was the photo that Rachel's mother had given him at the funeral. His eyes were mesmerised by hers once more. Those beautiful hazel eyes pleaded with him from the past. He remembered exactly how he had felt in that moment they had met, and suddenly he realised, through her, that the truth was owed. He looked at Scott in the dock. He resolved to tell the truth. The prosecutor repeated his question. He took a deep breath and steeled himself.

'No.'

'*What?*' The prosecutor was beside himself. 'I don't think you understood the question.'

'I did. And the answer is no. It wasn't premeditated.'

'I have your statement here and it clearly indicates that you believe that Scott Fowler murdered Rachel Robinson, in retaliation for her affair with you.'

'I was confused.' No, Charlie, tell the truth. He corrected himself. 'I lied. I was angry and grieving and I wanted Scott put away forever. I was wrong.' He felt sorry for the prosecutor and added, 'I'm sorry.'

The prosecutor turned a humiliated shade of scarlet and faced the judge. 'No further questions, your honour.'

Charlie was whisked out of the room and the court burst into murmured frenzy. The media furiously tapped at their BlackBerrys as the judge appealed for silence and addressed the jury.

'You have heard the evidence and now you must retire

to make your decision. Court adjourned.' Bang went the gavel.

It didn't take long – it was an hour at most before the jury were ready with their verdict. I returned to watch the outcome. Scott's lawyer was whispering words of encouragement to him and he was nodding sagely. I tried to work out what my feelings were towards him and with a jolt I realised I didn't have any. But still I needed to know the outcome of the trial. The judge addressed the foreman, 'You have, after careful consideration of the facts, reached a unanimous verdict?'

'We have.'

'For the charge of inciting racial hatred, how do you find the defendant?'

'Guilty.'

'For the charge of assaulting a police officer, how do you find the defendant?'

'Guilty.'

'For the charge of attempted murder, how do you find the defendant?'

'Guilty.'

'For the charge of murder, how do you find the defendant?'

'Not guilty.'

'For the charge of manslaughter, how do you find the defendant?'

'Guilty.'

And that was that. Scott's face was inscrutable. The judge's too. 'You will return in one month for sentencing.' Bang went the gavel.

Scott was sitting on the bunk of his holding cell when the guard announced he had a visitor and Charlie walked in.

'Why d'you do it?' Scott looked at Charlie curiously without getting up from the bunk.

'Because I was there and in my heart of hearts I know it was a mistake. And I know that the blame cannot fall entirely on your shoulders. You pulled the trigger but we all failed her and me most of all.'

Scott betrayed no emotion but then he looked down and in the moments before he looked up again, his eyes had filled with tears.

'I'm so sorry,' he said. 'I don't know how it happened. One day I was the happiest man alive – and the next, things fell apart. I never meant to take Rachel with me.'

'I know you loved her too…'

'I did.' Scott swallowed hard, 'But I became incapable of really showing it to her. It's hard to love wholly when other things are getting at you. I was so angry.' He looked directly at Charlie and repeated, 'I'm so sorry.'

'I need to know something,' Charlie said tersely. 'A year or two ago, Rachel had a black eye one time. Was it you?'

Scott shook his head urgently. 'No, I never laid a finger on Rach, I promise. I remember it though – she slipped in the kitchen.'

Charlie believed him and felt slightly better. He asked somewhat cruelly, 'So what now for you?'

'Well, I've got plenty of time to think it over. But I'm not angry any more. I'm just sorry. I can never make amends but I can still try to do some good, however little. I'm gonna be rehabilitated,' he announced.

Charlie nodded and felt an awed respect for Scott's determination to try again. Harder. Better. There was a presence of peace about him as if Rachel had spoken to him and had forgiven him. Scott spoke once more.

'So what about you?'

'Got a job in London at my Dad's bank.'

Scott's face screwed up in bafflement. 'Really?'

'Yeah, why?'

'Well, it's just I always thought,' he gulped before mentioning the name, 'Rachel always told me that you were planning to fly off somewhere and do charity work or some shit.'

'Plans change,' said Charlie simply.

'You twat.'

'I'm getting a little sick of hearing that.'

'You're giving up, aren't you? Taking the easy route… Daddy's got you a job.'

'I don't know why everybody's berating me for starting a fucking career and straightening my life out.'

'Because you're giving up, dickhead. You're falling through on yourself.'

'Fuck that, no I'm not. I'm starting afresh.'

'Nah,' Scott shook his head dismissively. 'You're a coward. And Rachel would think so too.'

Fire raced into Charlie's angry eyes and he slammed his palm against the door and called for the guard. He refused to listen. Scott watched him walk out the door with studied disappointment and he met Charlie's eyes as he looked back in anger.

His Dad was waiting for him in the car park. Charlie jumped into the passenger seat.

'Right,' he said. 'Let's go.' James Dixon started the car and they began to head back down south.

CHAPTER FOURTEEN

You know how it is at Christmas. Interminably damn boring. When life has beaten you so relentlessly into submission and the will to fight is sapped. Gone. The human spirit is broken. Mangled. Charlie was unerringly polite that Christmas. Unendurably helpful. He spoke when spoken to – hollow words designed to tickle the ears of his parents.

Jesus *Christ*! Where are you now, eh? We're still celebrating your birth and ignoring the fact that you're dead. Gone. Kaput. The absurdity of hope. For the fallen? Or the falling? Who the fuck even cares?

Charlie, Charlie, Charlie. What utter bollocks you pathetic self-pitying fool. Why don't you try? I know there's some courage there deep down and I won't give up on you but snap the fuck out of it. Now!

But he never listens and throughout that Christmas day he shoulders his heavy heart and bleeds invisible tears for yesterday in the shadowy depths of his pupils. He's moving on though. His father watches him at lunch and notes with pride how his clean-shaven, once brazen son touches not a drop of alcohol. Why would he? There is nothing left to numb.

Christine, his mother, is uneasy. She knows her husband has mistaken capitulation for determination but she resigns herself to the fact and mourns internally for her boy's broken dreams, his shattered heart. She hopes that time might heal him.

On New Year's Eve, Charlie smiled from time to time as he realised that his withdrawal from drugs had been supported by the leftover food from Christmas dinner. Cold turkey sandwiches to be precise. But he didn't have the heart to fall about laughing at this irony.

Self-pity, which had plagued him throughout his life, had killed his sense of humour. I'm not trivialising his sorrows – to lose a love is a terrible thing but come on, how's that for irony? Cold bloody turkey!

Still, loss is a terrible thing. It consumes our thoughts and minds and thus our sense of the absurd – a vital tool in this confusing world and when faith is absent, an essential weapon against the relentless futility of grief.

All other emotions have been dulled for Charlie for a while now because grief has consumed them all. So he doesn't really take things in. When his father tells him that on New Year's Day, tomorrow in fact, they would be going into the bank together so Charlie could be shown the ropes and shown around, he grunts in acquiescence, goes to kiss his mother goodnight, and retreats to the refuge of his room.

This is just how it's going to be, he figures. This veil of doom will never lift. But I'm optimistic. Nothing lasts forever and something or someone will surely soon assail him with joy. Or am I falling for clichés, gentle reader? Are you?

And the question begs to be asked. What do we owe to those who we've loved and lost? If to those whom we love and who live we owe the truth, then to those who have gone on, we owe the courage to go on too. Alone. For surely this is what they would want.

But Charlie has given up. He's fallen apart. He hasn't

190

ever really tried and on this night, at the end of this decadent decade, he hopes that slumber will rescue him from thought.

But sleep failed to rescue Charlie and he lay awake all night. Pain furiously hunted thoughts, fears and memories through the debris of his mind. They were long hours that preceded the dim, bleak sunrise of 2010 and when it grudgingly arrived, Charlie began routine. Zombie-like, he walked downstairs, picked up the newspaper, went to the kitchen and prepared breakfast. A cup of black coffee from the coffee-making machine. Two slices of brown bread with low-cholesterol butter. He looked fleetingly at the paper and the pictures of New Year celebrations and threw it to the floor in disgust.

He showered for exactly five minutes and began to get dressed. He took his only suit from the wardrobe, still unwashed since the funeral, and he pulled it over a plain white shirt. He chose the same black tie he had worn that same sad day.

He wound the noose around his neck and began to tie the Windsor knot he had been taught so long before. Remembering suddenly, he pulled from the inside pocket of his jacket the picture that Rachel's mother had given to him at the funeral of the night they had first met. And as he fingered the old, battered photograph, his pain and defeat forced him to drag his gaze away from those beautiful hazel eyes. He noticed for the first time the dumb yellow slogan emblazoned across the front of her shirt that night his life began. It read:

OUR
LOVE
STORY

191

He recognised the cruel and brutal irony of the story's author. The omnipotent author of life, who had penned but a prelude before abandoning his work as the life drained out of Rachel in Charlie's cradled arms.

He let out the briefest of bitter laughs and tied tight the knot of her betrayal.

ACKNOWLEDGEMENTS

I owe a significant debt to those who have helped with this book at various stages. My family have been as incredible as they always are, but I would also like to thank the following people for their support: Algernon Trotter, Rachel Cakebread, Jenny Hazan and Vicki McKendrick-Ness for reading early drafts; Ray Robinson at The Literary Consultancy and Joanna Lawson and Liz Hughes for their proof reading prowess.

And of course you, the reader, if you managed to get this far!

David Couldrey, London 2012.